Moving On

Maria Matthews

Illustration by: Constantinos Thersippos Karentzos
"Field", a digital sketch of an original artwork,
with model Sofia Doulgeraki

To Pat, Sara, Niall, Leo, Kate, Moira,
Bob and Ellie.

Thank you Betsy Lu
for your support
& kind words of
encouragement.

Maria Matthews
& Bob!

1. The Race

"Hike on," Ally shouted, leaning forward against the blast of wind as her team of four Irish sled dogs bounced into top speed pulling her around the steep bend. Their waving tails declared, to those watching the race, their love for doing this work.

She wondered if they would run well across snow. It would make a welcome change from sludge and muck. Running on snow was a dream. Ally wondered about it for a second while noting the amount of muck on the track. In comparison the countryside around her looked green and beautiful but Ally hadn't time for artistic appreciation. She was here to win.

Shouts of encouragement mingled with the barking of chasing teams reminded her every competitor wanted to win. Once more she asked her team to accelerate. With their thick double coats gleaming in weak Irish sunlight, they obeyed her shout.

"We are all in this together. I won't let you down," she promised.

Despite cold air and dirt being kicked up in her face Ally smiled. Luna was lead dog today. Excited noisy barking behind alerted them, another team was getting closer. Luna turned her head to peep back, her dark eyes gleaming. She didn't need encouragement from Ally to pull harder.

The last hill loomed ahead, a mere pimple in the distance. The wheels of her rig slid all over the track, Ally knew what to do. She jumped off and ran hard, pushing the rig with all her strength. The thin wheels of the rig bounced about making it difficult to keep a grip on the bar. It was tough to keep up with the dogs. Far behind she could hear a male voice roaring abuse at his dogs. She flinched, recognising the voice but also remembering how John, her ex husband loved to shout. Ally treated her dogs like most things in her life, with gentleness and persuasion.

"Focus Ally." she whispered knowing this was not the time to dwell on anything but what she had to do.

It was tough not to think of a portion of her past while she was racing. Sam, her father, had introduced her to this sport when she was a feisty teenager. Moving home, because of his illness, was the best decision of her life. She owed everything to Sam. In contrast, she owed John, nothing. Sam's death had left her feeling isolated and alone.

The biting wind caused her to shiver and pulled her back to the present. Chewing on her bottom lip, she lifted her head. 'We need to get up and over this damn hill if we are to win.' With a roar of encouragement she pushed even harder. Like her dogs, she was prepared to put every last ounce of energy into the race. Once they gave their best, Ally was happy. Hands firmly on the bar before her, she pushed as though her life depended on it. Her feet slid about on the wet heavy ground, making her feel as though she were carrying two buckets of sludge. Her breath came in gasps leaving her ribs aching as she continued to push.

She reached the top, took a deep breath to help prepare her for the treacherous down slope. Jumping back on, she applied light pressure to the brake with her right foot. Ally encouraged them to hold back. "Slow up, Luna," she shouted.

Droplets of water splashed her as she brushed against coniferous branches lining the steep path. She ignored the wet patch spreading between her shoulder blades. Ally focused on the track ahead, aware of the mix of human voice and dogs barking behind them as they edged closer to her team. She wondered who was catching them. She smiled, 'doesn't matter, we will win.'

Arriving at the bottom of the hill in one piece, she had time to notice grey clouds lifting marginally, the sun attempting once again to shine. Her spirits soared until she glanced behind her.

It was Steve, a rival, who didn't like being beaten especially by a woman. Behind him she saw a sparkling new rig with a shiny new competitor on board. Though his dogs were big and gaining on her, Ally hoped her experience would gain her the upper hand.

The track was level. The outside of it was hard while the inside track, looked to be in a similar state, but was wet and boggy. Ally knew what to do. In a minute she would discover if Steve knew the course.

He closed up on her. As his dogs came alongside hers, Ally pulled further right. She was as far to the outside as she could get.

He saw her move and grinned taking the inside track. His grin became a smug leer.

Ally acknowledged his mistake with a small smile of her own. She had just beaten him by her knowledge of the track. Steve didn't know it yet. He believed she was pulling back, letting the stronger team pull ahead.

She grinned and chuckled. 'If you think I quit that easily you are a mug Steve. You have a lot to learn.'

His mistake surprised her. She knew he was rough with his dogs, now she added arrogant to the list. Her guess was he had not bothered to walk the track as she had earlier. 'Well, sometimes the best way to learn is the hard way.' It was harsh but it was the truth. It reminded her of how awful she had been at making life-changing decisions.

To her surprise the new team were close behind them. They, too, attempted to pull to the inside. As he drew level with her team, he shouted above the wind and howling dogs. "Thank you, honey. We appreciate being let through." His

3

deep husky voice carried easily in the wind. She ignored the comment. His sunglasses, she noted were as trendy as his flash clothes.

'I'm not your honey,' she thought. Ally bent her head, rounded her shoulders and dug deep as she encouraged her dogs to give chase.

"Hike on Luna. Hike on." Luna responded swiftly, as did her team. Ally smiled, thinking to herself, 'you may be small but you sure can sprint! And he is about to find out how fast we can go.'

In comparison her companion's dogs were sinking in the soft mud hidden on the inside of the track. It slowed them sufficiently. Ally recognized that the newcomer's team were fighting each other rather than working together. Luna sped by her eyes focused on the prize ahead.

Steve's dogs were tired and sliding on the downhill run. He urged them on with a crack of a whip. Then, as she drew level with him, there was another strong crack followed by a moment of stabbing pain. The whip hit Ally's right hand. Tears flowed but she kept her hand stuck to the bar. The roar of protest from the man behind her drifted away in the wind as Ally continued on.

She raced by Steve hoping he wouldn't take her victory out on his dogs later. Luna stretched out her thin frame as did the others and both men's teams were left floundering in the soft sticky ground.

Ally passed the finishing line thinking, 'we did it, Dad. I hope you were watching.'

She wondered what her other competitors would think about her win. They had been quick to dismiss her chances earlier. At the starting line two of them had looked scathingly at her team of two Siberian Huskies and two crossbred dogs.

A particular comment had hit her squarely between the shoulders. "Aren't your dogs a bit small, love? Maybe you should go home and leave this to the professionals."

Ally had ignored them. Eyes fixed ahead of her she focused on listening for the starting horn.

It hadn't helped her popularity when she crossed the finish line in second place in her last race. The prizes today were vouchers for dog supply shops. Keeping four racing dogs and one chunky one didn't come cheap. In Ally's world, every cent counted.

She smiled. It would be interesting to hear what those competitors who dismissed her earlier would say about her now.

2. The Meeting

A shout of delight announced the arrival of the third place team across the finish line. Ally noted his happiness and could appreciate how well he had done. She suspected he would have preferred to finish in first place. Taking a deep breath she walked forward in her usual energetic bouncy manner towards Steve. She decided to disregard her stinging hand. She couldn't prove he had intended to hit her.

Hand outstretched she congratulated him. He ignored her offered hand, saying, "You were lucky this time."

Ally nodded at him and turned away. She had expected no more from him. She could see the third prize winner breathless and smiling making a fuss of his dogs. He was new to racing but she had the odd sensation that they had met before.

Steve's next words brought her attention hurtling back to him."Racing is no place for a woman, but if you were looking for attention to get your dogs noticed. It worked. I'll take your lead dog off your hands. She is the best of an okay lot. "

She acknowledged his words with a cool tone in her reply. "I'm not asking for anyone to take any one of my dogs, off my hands, as you so sweetly put it. And they are much better than okay."

His next words put a chill racing through her, "I'll wait, you will be glad of the money soon enough but I won't make as generous an offer the next time. It was a lucky win. You and I know that."

With his comment swirling in her head Ally said, "Hmm. I suppose it was down to luck that I walked the route earlier and got thoroughly soaked. You should know conditions can change in a few minutes depending on weather and how many races are run before ours."

His expression became sterner. He moved closer. He towered over her as he began, "now look here."

He got no further because a smooth warm voice interrupted Steve saying, "I didn't realise this was a contact sport. If you are looking for an opponent, next time please make an appointment with me. I'd be happy to knock some sense and manners into you, Steve."

Ally watching Steve's face recognised the dangerous gleam in his eyes. She looked at the newcomer. She wasn't prepared for the cold calculating look in his eyes. Turning to Ally he said with a warm smile, "She's one smart, fast dog and you handled your team like a professional. I, on the other hand, made a mess of the last kilometre especially that bend."

Steve looked at him and grunted, "Great Tom. You know nothing. Just you remember what we talked about before." He turned on his heel and left them.

Shoving his sunglasses to the top of his head the man before her said, 'Now the oaf has left let's start again. Thanks for a great race. I'm Tom Lynch and I really enjoyed that. It was exhilarating.'

Her cold hand was enfolded in his large warm hand. As they shook hands a ripple of energy coursed through her causing her to let her hand drop from his. Looking up at him Ally discovered she was being watched by the darkest pair of eyes she had ever seen.

"I look forward to racing you again and I hope it will be soon." Tom said leaning towards her.

Ally felt she might be swallowed up by those eyes. She opened her mouth but didn't get a chance to reply because the moment was lost as she was surrounded by a group of older men who were loudly congratulating her on her win.

She was aware of Tom standing to one side listening to the murmurs of, 'well done Ally love,' and "you have done Sam proud. Good girl." Then she forgot everything. The mention of Sam's name brought tears to her eyes. Ally noticed some of the men wiping their own eyes as they turned away. Ally's dad, Sam, had been respected and loved in this racing world. She missed him, but racing brought his memory closer to her.

"May I offer my sincerest sympathy?" Tom's voice was soft but she jumped when he spoke, for a moment she had forgotten him.

The warmth and sincerity in his voice got to her. Ally blinking furiously to dispel the further rush of tears, nodded her head. "Thanks. He got me into this mess in the first place." All about them people were busy, shouting instructions to others or to barking dogs.

Tom kicked at a tuft of grass at his feet as he said, "Me too. I came to watch a race and met Sam. His enthusiasm encouraged me to pull Mac off the sidelines. He gave me a lot. Tips, advice and his time."

As he spoke his team had her attention. Ally chewed on her bottom lip waiting for a break in conversation to give him the bad news. She managed to suppress a grin when she saw two of them chewing through their shiny new harness. Her words sharper than she intended, "I think you should rescue your gear. They appear to like the taste."

Tom glanced behind him and groaned. He was moving towards them as he said, "Thank you and again, I'm sorry about Sam. Watch out for us next time. I'll be looking for you."

Ally dripping mud and water looked towards her team who were in a mucky but happy state. She walked over to them. After giving each dog a hug and praising them Ally became aware that one was missing: Bob.

She hadn't seen him sitting at the finish line with Bill, her father's best friend. Puzzled, Ally went in search of her team cheerleader. She discovered he had ditched Bill. Bob was sitting under a golf umbrella, with a lady. Ally noting her grey hair and twinkling eyes and gentle way of speaking to the dog, groaned. He had gained another fan.

The lady was enjoying a drink and a sandwich. Bob, Ally noticed, was being very attentive and appreciative. A sandwich was placed before him. He carefully inspected it, nudging aside the top layer of bread. Thin slices of cucumber and ham were swallowed in a hurry when he saw Ally thundering his way.

"I told you not to go around begging. Bob, what am I going to do with you? Can't I leave you for a moment? Bill was minding you, what happened?" Ally paused to glance at Bob's hostess.

"I'm sorry. It's my fault, I fed him. You look tired and wet. Would you like some tea?" Bob's new friend sounded concerned.

"No, thank you." Ally gritted her teeth and reminded herself to be polite. After all, this lady knew nothing about her wayward dog's love of begging.

"Bill had a job to do. He asked us to keep each other company. I do think you are being a bit hard on Bob. He has been great fun while my son deserted me to chase some woman or dogs. You know what men are like, always chasing something." She smiled at Ally. With a flick of her thin wrist she apologized, "Bob reminds me of him. So handsome that you can't refuse anything he asks. Please don't scold Bob. He's a child; look at those soulful sad eyes."

Ally remembered her manners. "Thank you for minding him. However he's a bold child. We must go. Come on Bob, up and at 'em." She didn't have to say another word, the dog got to his feet with difficulty and lumbered after her. Ally turned to him and said, "I hope the cucumber gives you trouble. You deserve it."

His loud belch ended the conversation.

3. A Normal Day

It was six thirty when Ally hauled herself from bed the following morning. A glance in her bathroom mirror made her grimace. Her restless night had worked its magic leaving her wavy brown hair in a tangled mess. She blew stray tendrils of hair from her grey eyes and contemplated the freckles, stark against her pale skin. 'I look a mess', Ally decided adding, 'I wonder if I have time for a haircut at lunchtime?'

Another glance convinced her it was a necessity. Pulling her wayward hair into a high ponytail she concentrated on getting her day started.

Her life had flipped upside down when her dad became ill. The dogs had been his venture. He loved training and racing them. When he was too ill to do this Ally took over. She loved being busy and often thought she was living the perfect life for her.

She did not regret leaving her husband. When they were married John had disagreed with her hobby believing she was throwing money away. She foolishly stopped racing. Ally cursed her stupidity in marrying someone who was so alien to her, in thought, deed and action.

Their marriage lasted a year. This had shaken her to the core because she grew up believing marriage was for life. After their first anniversary she realised neither of them would change. It was time to admit defeat.

Their last conversation as a couple, in her father's house, had been a gem. Luckily, Sam had been asleep in his room and never heard them.

"Why can't you make up your mind, Alison? I would love a direct answer from you, for once." His thick brows forming one black line above his eyes served as a warning to Ally. She bit her lip and looked from the five anxious faces outside in the yard to his sour one.

His eyes were lasers, piercing her. "You should come home with me now."

"No, I can't. I am needed here."

"You, Alison, are my wife. I expect you to listen and obey me." His closed fist hit off his thigh to add force to his words.

"Yes, I am. I believed our marriage would be a partnership, which it is not. John the truth is you don't want a partner." She hated to admit defeat but it was time for honesty. She was tired of John's selfish demands. With her dad ill she had hoped John might change his ways and help her.

The dogs hearing loud voices within were pacing, whining and muttering. The sky darkened, to match all their moods. She cast another glance outside. He noticed.

"It's those damn dogs. You think more of them. I want you to come home with me now. You can visit Sam every day."

She stared at him. Ally couldn't believe what she was hearing, Sam couldn't get out of bed without help, how could she think of walking away, turning her back on him. Taking a deep breath she tried to calm John perhaps then he would be compassionate.

"John please be reasonable, stop creating extra problems. For once, think of Sam,' Ally pleaded with him. She suspected it was his reputation he was worried about. It wouldn't look if friends of his suspected Ally had left John.

"We are agreed we have nothing in common. Now you are putting your father before me, sounds as though you have washed your hands of our marriage."The veins in his forehead were apparent. He turned from her, stared outside. When he

11

turned back the fire hadn't left his eyes though his voice was softer. "Alison, I'm telling you to come back with me."

Her answer was honest. "How can I leave him when he is ill?"

"I will expect you by six thirty or not at all." John stormed out of the house leaving her shaking with anger and frustration. He rang the following day asking her to take her belongings out of the house, preferably when he was not there. To add insult to injury he asked for her keys of the house.

Since then the only time they met was at her father's funeral. The meeting had been awkward for both of them.

Ally's life was focused on her inheritance - the dogs. She didn't regret one minute of the constant work attached to minding them.

Pulling on an old tracksuit and a comfortable pair of boots she set about her pre work morning routine. Four dogs all vied for attention. She knew Bob was moping waiting for hugs and attention. His new admirer was correct, he was like a child, and if Ally failed to make up with him after an argument he stayed out of her way. When she could stand him ignoring her no longer, she went in search of Bob. He was curled up in his kennel.

She smiled. This was a strong indication of him being annoyed at her. The large dog never slept indoors. He loved being outside, heat wave or minus twenty degrees made no difference to him. He adored being able to lie and simply absorb the goings on in the large garden around him. Bending down she reached into the kennel. Putting her arms about him, she gave him a hug, and whispered, "how about a bit of bacon for breakfast?" He snuggled into her, his wet tongue washed her face to seal the deal.

On the way into the house she went to collect the post. Recognizing John's handwriting, Ally was tempted to shove it in a drawer and forget it had arrived, but she knew curiosity would win and she opened it. It was as she suspected, a curt note asking for a divorce. She shoved it into her pocket and went to the fridge to get her most lovable but inactive dog his bit of bacon.

The ring of her phone interrupted Ally as she got into the car. It was Elaine, who worked with Ally. "I'm early for once Ally. I will pick you up is that okay?"

"Thanks Elaine but I'm in the car. See you in a minute." Ally needed to do something to distract her from John's letter.

Elaine got into the car and began to talk non-stop about her brilliant performance in the road race. Elaine could keep up and even outrun most of the kids they taught. She admitted during the killing of a bottle of wine one evening that she was doing okay for a woman who participated in the under thirty-five race category.

Today Ally let her friend's chatter wash over her. She couldn't dismiss John's note.

Elaine noticed. "What's up? You are exceptionally quiet this morning. How did the race go? Did you meet any dishy men?"

Ally answered the questions quickly. "Nothing's up. I'm tired. As a winner of my category race should be. I didn't meet any dishy men just a very irritating one. He could have been in an ad for toothpaste, shiny new clothes and all. Don't worry I sorted out his squeaky clean clothes. Remember, I am off men."

With a toss of her red hair, Elaine declared, "Rubbish. You can't be off men." Then silence for half a beat until the full meaning of Ally's words struck home. "You won. You won?"

Ally forced a grin. "I did." She bit hard on her bottom lip. She grimaced realising she was drawing blood. She tried to figure out why she didn't tell Elaine the full story about Steve and the annoying man jumping to her rescue and the woman she suspected was his mother. Her assumption was based on spotting them leave together in a black jeep with a matching black trailer behind it.

"Well done." Elaine looked over at her friend noticed the bleeding lip and asked, "Why don't you look extraordinarily happy? Leave your lip alone, here is a tissue."

Ally could see the concern in Elaine's eyes and she attempted to reassure her friend. "Yes, thanks, I am happy. I am amazingly tired but happy." Ally was, finding it hard to forget Tom's dark brown eyes.

"What are we doing this afternoon to celebrate?"

"We, as in you and me, are doing nothing. I am a different matter entirely. I have a lot of fish to catch or fry and the first is at lunch time."

Mention food to Elaine and she would always go in search of some. Today she pulled a bag of nuts and raisins, out of a carrier bag. "Sorry, I'm starving. Must be all the calories I burned last night. I went to the new gym and tried Zumba dancing. Ouch." She moved about in her seat trying to get more comfortable. Offering the bag to Ally she asked, "What is going on inside that head of yours? I know there is something bothering you. And before you ask I know this because you have not eaten one bit of chocolate since we started out this morning just your bottom lip."

Ally remained silent, considering if she should talk about it now or leave it for a while. Elaine would pull it out of Ally eventually, no matter how hard she tried to keep quiet. Ally phrased it gently, tactfully in her head, however when she opened her mouth, the words rushed out like air released from a balloon.

"I got a letter from John this morning. He wants a divorce in his words, now. Don't look at me like that. I am not reneging on my decision. Our marriage is over."

Taking her eyes off the road for a second Ally risked a sideways glance. Elaine was steadfastly munching her way through the bag of healthy treats.

"You know you are supposed to pick at those, not devour the whole packet in one sitting."

Elaine turned her radiant smile on Ally. "Yes, but I have a feeling I may be eating for two." Her giggling increased because of the expression on Ally's face. "No, not pregnant you dope. I'm eating for you and me. Because when you worry, you stop eating and lose weight. Mind you I wish I could lose weight."

Distracted by a car driver in front of them, who jammed his foot on the brakes, Ally lost track of their conversation. When the car moved on she tried to keep up with Elaine's way of thinking. "What are we talking about?"

Giving a dramatic sigh Elaine said, "You were about to talk about John's letter. Come on spill, you will feel better."

"Ah. We've arrived. We can talk on the way home. I need a distraction now."

Elaine looked at their surroundings, "I suspect we are in the right place for that."

Glancing out of the car window at the small school sitting amongst a large housing estate Ally was inclined to agree. When she opened the car door, noise of children playing in the schoolyard was deafening but welcoming.

4. School Work

Together, Ally and Elaine hauled the sports equipment out of the car and left it inside the schoolyard wall. Their movements were monitored by a group of scathing children who were sitting on a rough wall. Two of the children were chewing gum in an attempt to look cool. Neither woman opened their mouth to acknowledge them. They knew this group of eleven or twelve year olds would regret not offering to help later.

The entrance door swung open. A tall grey haired man raced out to meet them. With hand outstretched he greeted them, "Hi, you must be Ally and Elaine. Pleased to meet you I am Henry Stevens, principal of the school," picking up the nearest equipment bag he told them to follow him as he led the way into the warm school. "The canteen is the third door on the left, the bathrooms are further along the hall and here we are the hall." He pushed the door open and stood back to let them enter.

Once he deposited them and their equipment inside, he left them alone after saying, "Ten minutes - will that be long enough for you to set up and prepare for the onslaught?" Before they could nod their heads in agreement he was gone.

They lost no time in assembling an obstacle course on one side of the hall. On the other side they put out long jump mats and throwing equipment. Standing back Elaine surveyed their work. "Even if I say so, it is a piece of art."

The door swung open to announce the arrival of a chattering bouncing group of children. For the next hour and a half they put the group through their paces. Elaine gave her demonstration through the obstacle course, grinning when she received a round of applause.

At five to eleven they set off for the canteen, which, like the hall, was huge. The staff plied them with questions about how to keep the children busy during PE. Before they knew it, the bell was ringing to signal the end of break. With a sigh of regret that break and eating time was over, Elaine and Ally set off to welcome the next class. An hour and a half later they were packing equipment back into the car when Elaine began her interrogation.

"As I said, John wants a divorce." Ally bluntly stated. "My problem is, I feel I will be dammed for all time. Ironic isn't it when my heart says, yes, Ally you will be better off on your own."

"You know my opinion, the quicker you are free of him the better. He messed up."

"Don't say that Elaine. It was my cock up too, if you remember."

"But for what length of time should you continue to condone a man who behaved like an ape from the day you met him? I never liked him."

Everyone knew John and Elaine never got on. A few weeks after Elaine met him, she pleaded with Ally to forget him. Ally pleaded true love.

Months into her marriage Ally confided her suspicion about John seeing someone else. Elaine wanted Ally to confront him or leave him. The trouble was no matter what Elaine said, Ally wanted to give marriage her best shot. All through their school days Ally had insisted when she married it would be for life. John, Ally believed was her soul mate.

It was painful for her to admit the truth, "The truth is I mistook lust for love. I was wrong, you were right."

"Divorce him. For your sanity you must put it behind you. Don't become another woman full of regrets existing in a lonely cut off world. Go out into the world as a free woman

17

and enjoy it with enthusiasm." Throwing a grin at Ally she continued in a dramatic tone, "Embrace the real Ally, your feminity, strength, zest for life now you have got rid..."

Ally interrupted her. "This is not an audition for a TV show. Calm down. I get your point."

Elaine wasn't so sure, "Promise me next time, you choose who you want as a partner. Take your time. Sample the goods. Don't be swayed by fancy words and promises."

Ally giggled. "Sample the goods. Oh Elaine, you are funny."

Elaine, for once in her life, did not make light of the situation. In her mind there was only one thing to do, divorce John and move on. Elaine knew Ally would do it, eventually. Sitting in the passenger seat, she turned to Ally and said, "Who knows what or who is around the corner for you? What happens if you stand back? Shit happens, or worse you become a mere spectator. Live each moment like it's your last."

When silence met this statement, Elaine leant towards Ally saying, "Promise me you will get advice before this whole messy process begins. I think you should go see a solicitor. Knowing your rights, will ensure you won't be talked, or bullied into agreeing to something you shouldn't have."

Driving into the office car park Ally promised she would, adding "today I think a trip to the hairdresser is important and then later, dinner."

The mention of food was enough to distract and reassure Elaine. Once they put all of the gear back in the storeroom they signed out and parted company each, driving off in different directions to two very different households.

5. Hair Today, Gone Tomorrow

Ally relaxed under the hot steaming water as her hair was washed. When Laura arrived with scissors in hand, Ally simply said, "I need at least three inches off it please." She paused, and said, "Laura, go for it. Chop it off please. Surprise me."

Ally let the chatter flow over her until the gossip got interesting. They were talking about a very hot guy with killer brown eyes. She glanced over at two young women having their hair cut.

"You have to admit, Breda, he must be nice. Not many men would come home to help their mum while she goes through her chemo. It shows a tender soft side to him. His two sisters could have coped." The young girl continued in a dreamy voice. "I wouldn't mind him taking care of me. Those eyes, that smile, he's perfect. I hear you have to join a queue."

Her friend, Breda giggled, "It's a long line of women. Though there are no complaints about him, so far." Lowering her voice a little, she continued, "Me, I think he came home because his business is in trouble."

"No, I think you are wrong. I think he is a strange man. He doesn't go to the local pub, just fancy restaurants and gorgeous women."

Breda smacked her lips together as she said, "Told you, a womaniser probably searching for a widow with loads of money of her own. Maybe he has no money."

"Rubbish. He must have money. He goes sled racing with dogs. It costs a lot of money to keep them. Strange hobby when we have no snow and the sled is on wheels. Like sitting on a bike being pulled by mad dogs. So why would you do it?"

There was a moment of silence as they considered the options. The answer was a statement, "I've no idea, makes no sense to me. I think he must be chasing some woman. I suppose he would get bored of women throwing themselves at him. He must have set himself a target."

Laura leant close to Ally and whispered, "No, they are both wrong. I heard he has obsessive, compulsive disorder and expects a lot from a woman. I've heard he is very competitive, he would do anything to win."

Hating herself for asking the question Ally said, "Do you know this ruthless man?"

"Oh, yes. Now if I was twenty years younger, I would teach him a thing or two. His name is Tom Lynch; he must be all of thirty five years of age. He is one of those trendy high flyers. He is: a man who gets what he wants."

Ally's heart sank. 'Why am I paying attention to gossip about a womaniser, who has a fan club?' Tom's dark brown eyes sprang to her mind. She dismissed them. 'I'm off men.'

"There you go Ally, I'm done. What do you think?" Laura asked.

Ally looked in the mirror and smiled as she swung her head left and right. "It's great. Thanks Laura."

Having paid and left, Ally smiled when she caught sight of her reflection in a shop window. It was a strange looking Ally staring back at her. Her new shorter choppy hairstyle made her eyes look huge. 'The dogs won't know me', she thought as she continued on her way home.

Of course they did.

6. Keeping Dogs Busy Invites Trouble

With no competitions ahead of them for weeks Ally could relax. Having changed from work wear into jumper and jeans, she set off for her dad's shed. She was searching for agility equipment, which he had made for Luna. The dog had to be kept busy and this had been Sam's answer.

Ally pulled the equipment out of the garage and set it up in the middle of the large back garden. She put Alex, the oldest dog in the team, running the course. He was diligently working his way through each piece of equipment when the impatient Luna broke free from Ally's grasp. She had forgotten the one golden rule; Luna could not wait in a queue.

Luna chased Alex across and around every piece. The tunnel was her favourite. When Luna saw Alex heading for it she decided to beat him to it. After pushing him out of the way and shooting through it; she raced about the garden barking with excitement.

With difficulty, Ally put Luna on a leash. Alex, Zoë and Butch went through the routine like three sedate housewives out for a morning's shopping. Luna barked loudly as though urging them to pick up the pace. This noisy event was watched with disdain by Bob, who never went over anything, unless there was the definite promise of food at the end of it.

When the three dogs were showing signs of boredom, she unleashed the storm from beside her. Luna bounded over the three jumps, raced up the A-frame; zig-zagged her way through the poles and trotted across the high walker. Luna paused for a second and pivoted about towards the tunnel. Ally smiled.

Luna raced towards it. Ally turned to Butch and whispered "Through Butch. Go through." The pure white husky calmly walked forward into the tunnel. Ally's eyes were fixed on it, to see who or what would emerge. Neither dog did. They remained within. When the barking grew intense, Butch emerged from the same side he had entered and trotted over to Ally. She gave him a treat and a rub under his chin. "Sorry, thought you might get to chase her for a change."

As Ally was speaking she became aware of how quiet it was. The afternoon was unusually warm. The four dogs were lying patiently at her feet panting rapidly. There was no sign of Luna.

Ally went to investigate. Bending down and crawling into the tunnel she caught a glimpse of her missing dog. She began trying to coax the dog out, but Luna was having none of it. It was far cooler inside the tunnel. And that was where they were when her caller arrived.

7. Tom Visits Ally

Tom found himself thinking of Ally a lot during his day. After he called his sister Caroline, Ally, by mistake, he was forced to explain who Ally was and how they met. He finished with a shrug saying, "She is a puzzling woman. I can't figure her out."

Caroline smiled, "That's a first for you. I think you should call on Ally. Do you know where she lives?"

His smile was sad. "I do. I met her dad. Sam passed away a while ago."

Caroline took a moment before speaking. She knew this was new territory for him. Tom never had to search out a woman, until now they always came to him. "Bring her a gift, every woman loves a gift."

The trouble was Ally didn't strike him as being a flower type of woman. Later that day Tom's thoughts turned to her again as he stood before the old rig he had learnt to race with. It was lent to him by Sam.

He smiled remembering Caroline's words. 'I'll simply return a rig.' Having loaded it into his trailer he went to get ready. Dressed, in snowy white shirt and clean jeans, he set off for her house. The level of noise that greeted him when he arrived was deafening. It sounded like a dog was fighting, or turning on something or someone.

Racing around the corner of the house the sight of what appeared to be Ally's very attractive rear end and legs sticking out of a twisted tunnel made him pause. Tom had no idea if she was hurt, dead or hiding

'If you are hiding you are not doing a very good job', he thought racing to her rescue. Dashing over to her was not easy with the dogs barking and dancing about him. With difficulty he struggled through the pack. Bending down he grabbed Ally's legs and yanked with all of his might.

"Hey! Let go! Elaine if it's you then you had best let me go. Besides I almost had the little brat." Ally, red faced, rolled over onto her back and stared up into a familiar pair of sparkling brown eyes.

As their eyes locked Tom knew from her glaring stare he was in trouble. Tearing his eyes away from her body he attempted to explain his actions. "Thank God you are ok. I thought something awful happened to you. All I could see was your bum and legs sticking out of the tunnel." Tom paused recognizing the glint of anger in her eyes. Ignoring the danger signs he finished with, "I have to admit it was a stunning picture," he twisted his head sideways, "whatever angle you looked. What the hell were you doing?"

"Never mind me. What are you doing? Who told you where I live?" Ally's ranting and raving died on her lips when she looked at his feet.

Tom followed her glance. His shoes were under attack from her guard dogs as they methodically licked his shoes. Next they moved onto his hands. They were fighting for his attention. He absently noted the garden was big enough to put two tennis courts on it. He wished he had a ball to throw to deflect their attention from him. Slobber was flying in all directions.

Tom grinned at her. He hoped for a thawing in her manner, but he suspected it wasn't happening. Her words confirmed his suspicion.

"Please answer the question, what brings you to my door?"

"Not door but garden. Nice greeting for your guest, by the way. I'm glad your dogs know how to treat a man."

"You are not my guest. You barged in." Ally stood hands on hips glaring at him.

He noticed she didn't try to pull the dogs away from him. Well, time to surprise her, he decided saying, "I came to return the chariot your dad gave me." He silently added 'I know, having two sisters, how women feel about stuff like this.'

He noticed the trembling lips and how she became busy fiddling with her hands. He cursed himself for messing up again. Her eyes were glazing over. He hoped she didn't cry because then he would give in to his overwhelming impulse to pull her into his arms. "I have it in the trailer. If you will give me a hand, I can get out of your hair, which looks amazing by the way," he said, knowing his sisters appreciated a truthful opinion.

"Ahh, you are a professional hairdresser as well as detective, toothpaste commercial guy, clothes model and dog handler?" Her words were coated in sarcasm.

Tom acknowledged he deserved it, intruding on her privacy, not to mention dragging her out of the tunnel, but he wasn't going to let her get away with labelling him.

"I object to being stereotyped. I mean how could you call me the toothpaste commercial guy?" He raised his eyebrows and continued speaking, "don't you think these too dazzling for TV?" He finished with a toothy grin. As they walked towards his jeep, he caught sight of their reflection; she looked tiny and fragile. Irrational, he knew, from all he was witnessing. She was one tough woman.

8. Return of a Gift Brings Memories and Tears

Following Tom out to his car Ally was swamped by a rush of emotions. She treasured everything belonging to Sam. She felt guilty because she hadn't noticed it was missing. Catching sight of herself in the jeep window she lamented the fact she looked tatty. Tom on the other hand, looked as though he had stepped from a magazine. Arriving at the jeep and trailer she lost all interest in Tom's appearance.

The sight of Sam's rig brought tears to her eyes. She remembered the happy times with Sam. How persistent he was she race again after she left John. She had objected to returning to race, believing she wasn't up to the job. He won her over. Her first day back racing had been tough. Sam had looked ill but insisted on going to watch and offer advice. She remembered it vividly; a warm sunny autumn day, trees whispering softly while her heart hammered loudly Ally supposed everyone could hear it.

"Will you kill me if one of the dogs gets injured?" She asked pulling on a pair of well-worn gloves. Her competitors seemed so professional in comparison to her.

Sam's grin had been wide. With one hand pointing at his chest he said, "More chance that you will be like your old man and hurt yourself first. But don't do that because I'd have to blame them and shoot every one of them, including Bob."

Bob, sitting beside Sam, turned his back on them to show his feelings on the subject. Ally giggled. She had started her race with a wobbly stomach. She survived, crossing the line in

26

the world records slowest time. What Ally hadn't banked on was the way she felt afterwards. With her blood pounding from the effort, her smile so bright, she felt she was the winner instead of the slowest racer of the day.

That first race back into the racing world did awaken her competitive streak long since buried by John and his habitual need for constant attention. Since that first day back at the reins she hadn't stopped.

With a start, she discovered Tom standing close to her. So close she could smell his aftershave and feel the whisper of his breath on her cheek. He was staring into her eyes, asking, "Are you alright? I didn't mean to upset you. I felt it was the right thing to do, to give it back, I mean."

Scrubbing the tears from her face, she nodded and said, "Just being sentimental that's all. Let's get her stashed away." As she spoke Ally turned to check on Luna. The dog was hidden in the middle of the tunnel where it was cool. With a shrug of her shoulders she said, "Isn't that typical? She stays cool while I get hot and bothered, worrying about her."

"As I said, she is one smart dog, if you ever think of quitting the game I'll..."

Ally cut him off saying, "You can forget that. We don't mention the quit word around here. We've all got the bug bad in this house, except for Bob. None of us will quit."

She was relieved when he agreed that it was an addictive sport and let the subject drop. It didn't take long to stow the rig into a corner in the shed. Tom wiped the dust from his hands, on his trouser legs, saying, "Now before I leave why don't we fix a time and date for dinner?"

"What?" Ally was remembering that big fan club thinking, I won't become a number in his book. She speculated on why he was asking her. While he slowly repeated his offer, she considered the number of times he had angered her this afternoon. First by simply appearing looking so pristine and charming, then by dragging her out by her legs, next he criticized her hair, implied she would quit racing and finally by demanding a date.

The return of the rig did win him a brownie point, but only one. He would need a whole basket full if he was to get in her good books, she decided noticing the intense way he was watching her. She felt a little sorry for him it was obvious from his droopy shoulders and quiet manner that he was aware of what a total mess he made of his invitation. She hoped he would give up easily. However, remembering the discussion in the hairdressers she suspected he would try another way around the problem. She didn't have long to speculate on how he would approach her.

"Well, how about this? I challenge you, Ally, to our own private race. I, the winner, will buy you dinner to celebrate."

She opened her mouth to scold him then paused to consider this option. She could use the practise and she would enjoy beating him again. Her anger was simmering as she answered, "I accept. You name the date and time. I'll be there. Huh, fat chance of you winning."

Unfortunately she realised her mistake when she noticed his bright smile. Ally pivoted about on her heel before she gave in to the urge to throw something at his smiling face. Then abruptly she swung back around to face him. "As for your forfeit, when I win: you have to mow all the knitting group's ladies lawns for two weeks."

"Easy, peasy. What shall we eat for dinner?"

"Humble pie." She wanted to kick him. He was so sure of himself. 'He may pluck another victim from his fan club for dinner' she decided, walking off and leaving him. She stopped at her back door and listened to the sound of his car starting. She hoped he was driving away with all of his hopes and aspirations towards her firmly squashed.

She couldn't relax instead Ally paced about the kitchen. 'What is wrong with me? Why do I attract crazy men?' She didn't linger on this but instead decided he was a modern day Casanova. A second later she did a u turn on that idea. Could it be about racing and winning? Maybe he was as competitive as she. With a sigh she decided to leave this mystery unsolved. "I am off men, in particular any roving tooth flashing Casanova looking for scalps to hang off his bedpost!"

An excited bark told her Luna was out of the tunnel, chasing the others in the garden. She decided to take advantage of them being preoccupied with each other to catch up on some dreaded housework.

9. In Mourning

During the next week Ally attempted to forget Tom. It worked until she spotted him accompanied by a very attractive lady in his car. Her blood pressure was rising as she speculated on how large a harem he had. She didn't know what irritated her more, him constantly appearing or the fact she noticed him so much.

Instead she focused on her divorce. It needed to be dealt with. Her marriage had been a mistake, but accepting this and moving on was very hard to do. Ally took out the telephone book and searched for a solicitor. There were a lot of them. She closed her eyes and ran a finger down the list, stopping suddenly. She opened her eyes and saw the name R.O'Connor.. "And off to Mr R. O'Connor I go." She said grabbing her keys. She knew if she stopped and thought she would find an excuse to put off the visit to the solicitor's office.

Along the way she became convinced it would be a simple matter, because they both wanted the divorce. Agree by signing some papers and that would be that. Instead Ally quickly learnt how formal and lengthy a procedure it would be.

On returning home she methodically started to work her way through the mountain of notes she had scribbled down during the hour-long discussion with a very nice polite elderly man. Then she turned to the forms. The first question was a sign of the times we are living in, she thought and read it again. Are you and your spouse living in the Republic of Ireland?

"Of course we are, or we would have got a quick divorce by now," she whispered.

With a sigh she glanced down the list. It wasn't a long document but she suspected being a legal paper it would be complicated. She was correct. They had to be living apart for a period of at least four years during the previous five years of their marriage.

'A tricky point given we were only married a year when we decided to part. And that was ten months ago, so we have a long way to go.' She worked her way through it methodically. The last sentence hurt: there is no reasonable prospect of reconciliation between the spouses.

She glanced quickly at the next paragraphs and dismissed them. Having no children was proving to be a blessing. In approximately two and a half years time she or John would have to attend or their local Circuit Court office with a bundle of papers under their arms. Amongst the list was a copy of the Family Law Civil Bill, An affidavit of Means (which meant in their case: their house). Then if everything were in order, the court office would "issue" the proceedings.

She learnt the documents provided by the court must be served within certain time frames and in a certain manner. "And then I will be a free woman again." Ally muttered getting up to put the paperwork away.

The doorbell rang at precisely that moment.

10. John

Ally was not impressed when she opened the door. John's opening comment aimed to hurt, didn't improve her humour. "Gosh, Ally, you look dreadful. Are you ill? I thought you were out, it took you so long to open the door."

His familiar aftershave was strong. It brought back many bad memories. Ally felt ill. Leaving the door open she turned away from him to walk into the kitchen. He followed. She switched the kettle on thinking, 'what I need most at this moment is a large cup of coffee.' Aloud she said, "To what do I owe the honour of this visit?"

He ignored her comment. "I see nothing has changed here. You were never one to consider change of any kind."

Ally counted to ten. Turning to face him she put a stiff smile on her face, "Tea, coffee or arsenic? Or would you prefer to stand there and deliver sweet nothings to me for the rest of the afternoon?"

His answering smile was swift and cold, "You know I like my coffee mild and sweet, like the women in my life." Running his finger along the table, he said, "Hmmm." He was rubbing imaginary dust from his fingers.

Ally busied herself making coffee. With reluctance she took out the biscuit tin, she had no inclination to delay or extend his visit by a second longer than was needed. Placing his mug before him, she sat noting without surprise, that his smile had the warmth of an iceberg.

"As I didn't hear from you I assumed you didn't receive my letter. I brought a copy for you." He was leaning towards her as he spoke.

"Thank you. I got it." Ally calmly took a drink from her mug. Noting the dark circles beneath his eyes she hoped his new girlfriend, Liz was being very demanding.

"And?" He smiled, in the confident manner she hated.

"And what?" She tilted her head and waited.

"I'm here to inform you of the terms of our divorce. I think, I should give you some help with it as I am told you are struggling at the moment."

It was the suggestive leering tone that alerted Ally. "Who says I am struggling?"

"I met an old friend of ours, Steve told me of his kind offer and your refusal to listen." His tone was placating, irritating.

Ally glared at him. She had forgotten Steve and John drank in the same pub. She wished she were Superwoman. She would pluck him from his chair and throw him out of her kitchen.

"Don't you think this whole situation is ironic given your firm belief in marriage? Especially since you were the one to leave." His eyes were fixed on her face.

Ally realised he was enjoying this. He obviously expected her to squirm and object to his suggestion. She remained silent.

"You have to see reason. Our marriage is over, divorce is next. It should be quick and painless." He continued speaking with a gloriously smug expression on his face, "I have moved on. I am in love with someone. You know I like to do things correctly." He paused hoping for shock at his announcement.

"I know." Ally calmly said.

"You know?" His eyebrows shot upwards.

Ally took her time about answering him. She calmly said, "I know about Liz."

It would have been tough not to know, as he took pleasure in flaunting his trophy girlfriend around the town. She was young, blonde and stunning.

Liz was the complete opposite of Ally. An image of an attractive lady sitting beside Tom flashed into her head. Ally focused on John.

"I have taken advice. You and I have to wait. The law states four years. With almost two gone you can begin your countdown, just two more and you will be free from me and I, blissfully from you."

John sighed. His relief was visible. He sat back in the chair. "I'm glad to see you are in agreement, it is time for us to move forward with our lives.

Ally let him bask in it for a moment. "Good, now there is the matter of the house." Ally paused before pulling her trump card, as suggested by her very kind solicitor. "I am not claiming support from you. Therefore I believe I should, and can, claim rent on the house."

His shout didn't startle her, "How ridiculous is that? Why should I?"

Ally remained seated and calm. "Why not? You and your girlfriend Liz are living in our house, jointly bought. Look at it from another angle. If you were not living in our house but living in Liz's place." She noted his flinch with a little glee. Liz, as Ally knew, didn't have a place. "We would put the house up for rent. I am paying half the mortgage."

"Ridiculous. She is my guest and it is my house." He was angered by this demand.

"Correction, it is our house and John she is not my guest."

"It is my house. I will not have a friend of mine pay rent to you. I say she doesn't have to and so she doesn't have to, end of story." His fist banged on the table, the mugs shook.

Ally remained cool. "If you have any queries or doubts about the legality of this, you can contact my solicitor. Here is the agreement and his details in case you need to talk to him."

Ally got up and taking the large brown envelope from the shelf placed it before John.

"I will not pay you one cent. Who put you up to this?" John spluttered, his colour changing from lightly tanned to firehouse red. "Why would you think of something so stupid? You have not heard the end of this from me. I will block this silly idea of yours. You do have another option if money is short. You could ring Steve accept his offer."

Ally gritted her teeth. Her hands were clenched, her eyes focused on the table. She refused to say another word. She counted to ten. When she felt calm she looked at him.

Getting up from her chair she opened the kitchen door saying, "I will leave it with you. Please don't contact me again. I don't wish to make this any more awkward or annoying than it has to be. Now if you don't mind I have an appointment with my beautician for my date tonight."

This statement threw him off balance, as she hoped it would. John jumped up from his chair and walked over to her. "You can't railroad me into something." He was marching past her. When he got to the front door he swung about, "I will fight you on this one." He stood glaring at her.

Ally picked up the envelope he had left on the table. "You should read it when you are calmer. I didn't expect anything else except a fight from you. Goodbye John."

Ally closed the door behind him. Feeling upset by the encounter she walked towards the kitchen. She needed to be outdoors. Whistling loudly she called the dogs to her and they set off for a long walk by the river. Their noisy company was a welcome distraction from the turmoil raging in her head.

11. Home Delivery Brings Suspicion

It was strange. Ally couldn't pinpoint her feelings. She didn't feel lonely just wished she were part of a big noisy family. Large and loud had at times been intimidating to her. There had been other occasions when she looked at her school friends with envy while they moaned about what a sister or brother had inflicted on them in the name of brotherly or sisterly love. It would be nice to have someone to ring to moan about John.

A slight gentle nudge in her knee alerted her. Looking down at her feet Ally saw a ball sitting on the ground. Four dogs waited for her, while the fifth sat apart with his head lying on his paws. Once she lobbed the ball as far away as she could Ally bent down and gave Bob a huge hug. His huff of contentment brought a smile to her face, with a shout of, "come on let's get them," she dragged him after the others.

Returning home Ally realised it was later than she supposed. She felt tired, too tired to cook. As she mixed up kibble with cooked chicken, for the dogs, she was tempted to swipe some of the chicken.

"I could make a salad or then again I could be not so good and have a big old fashioned cheese omelette." She told the audience at the back door.

As it turned out she didn't have to do anything. She fed the dogs and on her return trip to the kitchen noticed, a visitor entering by the side gate. Tom was walking with purpose towards her. She threw a cool glance his way hoping it would discourage him from lingering. Instead he pulled his shoulders back as though bracing for a storm. He walked towards her with a warm pleasant smile on his face.

Groaning she muttered, "Oh, great." She felt tired and her appearance was dishevelled. He, in comparison, was neat and tidy. In fact, he looked as though he might have been on his way for a photo shoot.

Ally tried not to dwell on Elaine's summary of him. Research had taken place in the village butchers shop, a reliable source, according to Elaine. The results were recited by Elaine; "a once successful business man whose business has downsized. He has lorry loads of women tripping over each other to get his attention. He is extremely competitive and always gets what he wants."

Ally realised Tom was speaking to her, "Nice way to talk to a person who decided to treat you to a taste of my cooking, should I leave with it?" With a flourish Tom swung the shopping bag he carried towards her.

Ally considered her options. Throw a man out, no matter how arrogant he is, or take advantage of the situation and eat? Her stomach answered for her.

12. Delivered with Intent

Tom was watching her, wondering what brought him back. He had no idea why he returned. He could have dialled one of many telephone numbers and be sitting in a swanky restaurant opposite a woman of manicured beauty.

Instead he was standing before Ally, who looked tired, hungry and cranky.

To his utter astonishment she said, "Dinner sounds great."

Stepping into the kitchen he became aware of two mugs sitting on the draining board and the lingering scent of strong aftershave. "Ah, you have company. I will leave this and go. I came to remind you that you have to pick Race Date Day."

"You mean the day on which I will beat you once more." Ally groaned and admitted. "I had forgotten all about the blasted race. Have you nothing else in life to worry about?"

Her sharp words left him debating if he should leave. It was obvious to him, Ally was anxious to be on her own with her first caller. He wondered if she had a secret life full of casual acquaintances all vying for her attention. To his surprise she blocked his way saying,

"Oh no, you don't. You can't come into a starving, exhausted woman's house with food, only to vanish as quickly as you arrive." Putting her hands on her hips, she made it appear as though she was issuing him with a challenge.

Stepping backwards Tom looked at her closely. "You don't look starving, merely upset." He looked at the mugs and back at her. His words didn't have the effect he wished for as she sank into a nearby chair. He noticed her frown and recalled Caroline and Sarah's advice, 'back off and take it easy,' when he related details of his last visit with Ally.

Moving back towards the table he left the carrier bag down and with a smile said, "take this in the spirit of friendship it is meant. Call me if you need anything. I apologise I cannot stay. I have to be somewhere else, I hope you enjoy it. My number is written on the carrier bag, though I might have been better to put the number for the hospital."

Tom quickly decided his sisters were correct in their assumption that she didn't like being crowded. From her astonished expression he guessed Ally was puzzled by the gesture and his words.

Before Ally could utter a word he left her standing there.

He hoped she didn't see the smile on his face. 'The girls will be proud of me,' was his sole thought as he left. Truth was he would have loved to stay and tease the tired worried look from Ally's face. However he was due to collect Tricia from hospital.

It was a small village and news travelled. Sarah knew of Ally's marriage and knew her husband John. She didn't mince her words when she described John to Tom. Her advice had been to be gentle give her loads of time.

Caroline wasn't so polite. "Go in there like they used to do in old films, sweep her off her feet carry her off into the sunset. Every woman dreams of such a moment. And you are perfect for the part, a handsome man with oodles of potential and no attachments."

Sarah and Tom roared with laughter as Caroline's husband was the most unromantic man on the planet. That conversation had led to him providing dinner for her. As he left he decided it was a good move.

Much later Tom sat in the hospital waiting room considering his problem. Steve O'Connor had approached him weeks before his first race with a request. Steve needed a lead dog. He explained to Tom how much he wanted Luna in his team but he suspected it would never happen for him because of a past disagreement with Ally.

Tom was in a sticky predicament. The deal was simple, buy Luna and sell her to Steve for a profit. Tom's problem stemmed from the fact that he was not a quitter. His struggle to keep his business going was testament to that. He was career driven but, at this moment he was floundering. Tom's original plan had been; meet Ally, make an offer and get out quick. That had been the game plan before Tom met Ally.

His excuse for agreeing to the deal was not pretty. Money was money and it was in short supply these days. The money would provide or open doors to a business opportunity. Not only would Steve pay him handsomely for getting Luna but he was willing to push some legitimate business Tom's way.

The trouble was it felt sneaky from the start and generally, he didn't do sneaky. In business or his personal life Tom was frank and honest. He always told the women he dated the truth. He wasn't interested in a complicated relationship or a life-long commitment, his business plan came first.

What Tom had not bargained on was the unknown force; Ally. She intrigued him. Worse, he was attracted to her. She gave off such mixed signals he had no idea where he stood with her.

From their first meeting Tom figured it would be interesting to be around her. What he quickly learnt was her dogs were like children to her. After returning the rig to Ally, he gave up on plans to buy Luna.

Today standing before her in the kitchen, his world tilted. He knew he would have to go back. This time the prospect of buying Luna or the proposed race between them would not be the magnet pulling him to her door.

Sitting in the over warm waiting room, Tom recognised how anxious he was feeling. He speculated on the chances of them becoming more than friends. 'Even if I were a gambler I wouldn't put money on it but I'm not finished yet.'

40

13. A Lonely Dinner and a Phone Call

Ally stood in the centre of the kitchen staring at the bag on the table. She opened the bag and took out a small tray of lasagne. Ally raised her eyebrows.

"It is an interesting choice but predictable." She said aloud as she emptied the contents on the table. There was garlic bread; a tub of mixed salad leaves, three baked potatoes wrapped in silver foil Ally's stomach was starting to rumble as the air filled with the scent of hot food.

Minutes later she was tucking into her solitary meal. An image of him as he met her outside gave her cause to wonder if his brown eyes ever stopped sparkling. The next question running about in her brain was; 'why had he come?' There had to be something other than a race behind it. I doubt if he wants to go out with grotty old me. Next time we meet I will dig it out of him.' She promised.

To stop dwelling on Tom's merits Ally focused on the poster pinned to her fridge door. She knew the wording by heart. The dog race would take place near Aberdeen. That meant finding the money to pay for travel and lodging. Then there was the matter of the entry fee of three hundred pounds sterling. Her phone rang at that moment.

"Hello," Ally mumbled her mouth full.

"You don't sound happy. Was dinner terrible?"

She groaned."Tom. How did you get my number?" Too late, she remembered she had given it to him at a weak moment after he returned the rig.

He didn't answer her question but asked, "Bet you were thinking of me as you ate dinner?"

She was tempted, to be flippant with him, a smart remark to avoid the truth. However she couldn't do that, he had brought dinner and, her dad's rig back. He deserved a polite answer. With a smile she said, "No. Sorry to disappoint you but I was thinking of the Aberdeen race, wondering how I could raise the money for it."

His words surprised her. "If money is an issue, then a sponsor could help."

Ally was quiet. A sponsor would be ideal her heart was pounding until he suggested, "I might be persuaded to help find you one."

"I don't need to persuade you for many reasons." Her tone was sharp. Ally had a good idea what type of persuasion he had in mind. Besides she was undecided about the race. She knew how difficult running on snow would be. Ally loved her one experience of snow in Ireland. Her dogs had adored it. But collecting, post, medicine and groceries for her elderly neighbours had been pure fun. The race would be tough. Other competitors would come prepared, with vast knowledge gained through years of experience.

She knew she sounded angry but she lived a real live, not one based on fashion and whims. She suspected he was not used to dealing with women like her.

Tom abruptly said, "Sorry. When you get to know me better perhaps you will reconsider my offer."

Ally was tired, and feeling bubbles of irritation rise within her she suspected it would be wiser to remain silent. When she did so, he wished her good night and ended the call.

14. A Chance Encounter

Ally walked out of the newsagents and bumped into Tom. His cheery grin didn't work on her. After a restless night she had decided, 'charming, confident men don't fall out of the sky and land on my doorstep for nothing, he wants something.'

The only thing she could think of saying was," I heard about your mum. I am sorry she is ill. I hope she is doing ok."

He faltered then his easy smile was back. "Yes, thanks."

Ally took a deep breath, "I suspect you are using all of this, the dogs, the racing and dinner to try to impress me. Why? I am not looking for a boyfriend, lover, or husband." As she spoke she watched his facial expression change from surprise and finally to puzzlement.

With a nod he said, "Okay. I am interested in you because of your knowledge of dogs and racing."

She didn't know how to reply to this, so decided to say nothing.

"I saw you racing. Sam pointed you out to me. I was impressed by the way your dogs responded to you. I was curious and wanted to know more, you know the rest." Tom crossed his fingers behind his back. Some of it was true. Sam had pointed Ally out to Tom. On the day in question she had been muffled up to protect herself from the cold wet day. Tom had caught a glimpse of her nose. A phone call from Tricia meant he didn't get to meet Ally on that occasion.

Ally wasn't convinced. He didn't look like a monster more like a small boy who was caught telling lie. She

43

wondered what else he was hiding from her. "I am curious though as to why you brought me dinner?"

She watched his eyes. He appeared to be weighing up the pros and cons of answering truthfully. She guessed she would only get to hear a little bit of the truth. She decided she didn't want to hear any half truths but he was already speaking.

"I was making amends for keeping your dad's rig for so long and also for manhandling you in the garden."

It was hard not to notice the way his eyes swept over her body. "Jack the Ripper could have delivered dinner. I would have entertained him and eaten his food with pleasure." She continued with, "I appreciate everything you have done, bringing me dinner, bringing back the old rig. The fact is I am not divorced, yet and more importantly, I feel married. I think I always will." Ally stopped. She had no wish to explain why she felt tied to John. It was too complicated. She was saddened by the guilt and burden of it all.

"I can only repeat what I told you. I am off men for life." She saw the droop of his shoulders and then noticed how he straightened up.

"Suits me, I am looking for a trainer, or at best a friend, nothing more, or less." Tom gently said. "Dinner was a gesture from one friend to another that is all. I didn't mean you to read so much into it. I can be a friend can't I? "

For some strange reason, her heart was tumbling about in her chest. She forgot to ask him why he was so interested in Luna. She left with the sickening feeling that he wouldn't give up. "Not good Ally, not good," she whispered.

15. Flu and Depression

Two days rolled by, work kept her going. If Elaine noticed Ally was not her usual self she didn't comment. Ally for her part knew she was depressed but couldn't do anything about it. Telling Tom about her divorce had triggered it. Her life was set in stone she couldn't or wouldn't trust men ever again. She would spend her life alone. She was trapped in a black hole and couldn't see a pinhole of light to guide her out. Inside she knew she would be far happier and better off without John however the reality of divorce was a shock to the system.

'Single and alone, I have nothing but you five,' she mused. She ploughed on through the days. The dogs were a comfort, a link to her dad. However, when she became ill with a nasty cold that headed straight to her chest, it was the last straw.

She wailed down the phone between sniffles. "I'm going to be late. I'm in the chemist buying every known drug to beat this blasted thing."

Elaine wanted Ally to go home. She refused so Elaine rang the school and rang her back again.

"I've told the school we will be late. I'll meet you in twenty minutes."

Sniffling and snorting Ally appeared in the office. Elaine looked up and grinned. "Why hello. Mrs Grinch isn't it? I don't believe we have met."

"Back off, show off, healthy fiend." Ally was clutching a hanky and carrying a bag of supplies from the chemist.

"Hmm don't you mean friend?" Elaine was sipping on a hot chocolate. As Ally glared back, Elaine reached across the desk and shoved a mug of hot chocolate into her friend's hands saying, "Bring it with you to drink. It will cheer you up. I even put marshmallows on top."

Ally sat in the car sipping on the drink. After a while she smiled. "Thanks, there is nothing like hot chocolate for making a woman feel more human."

"Only works if it has marshmallows on top and a swizzle stick. I asked myself earlier, which would Ally prefer, heaven in a cup or George Clooney? Did I choose the right one?"

Ally grinned. "Course you did. I mean how any woman could consider snuggling up to a man with a pig at his feet, no matter how gorgeous he is, it's beyond comprehension."

"Exactly. Now please read my coaching plan. Also note, that the same chocolate mug bearing friend has been very kind to sick Ally, and given her all the fun stuff to do."

Looking at the sheet of paper Ally refrained from making a comment. It looked as though ink had escaped from the biro and been blown about by a straw. "Why is there a stick figure standing in the middle pulling his hair out?"

"That is me. Don't you recognize the mad curly head of hair? I am doing drills, hurdles and ladders with my group. And we all know how much the kids love that stuff, don't we?"

An hour and a half later, Elaine was a hotter version of her picture. One of her team had refused to take part. Elaine issued a challenge, to see how many speed bounces the girl could achieve in twenty seconds. Ally was tempted to go and rescue her until she heard the verbal abuse given to Elaine.

On the way home the heat of the car and combination of the medicines made Ally drowsy. They were back at the office when she woke. "Gosh that was quick." When Elaine replied by raising an eyebrow and glancing at the clock Ally apologized. "I am sorry. I don't believe I slept through the whole forty minute trip."

Elaine made a clucking sound through her lips and announced, "That's fine, you look better. But I think more sleep is needed. I will bring you dinner later on. Go home, do the bare necessities and go to bed."

Ally did as ordered. She went home, rounded the dogs up and brought them in with her, then picked her favourite DVD, 'Pride and Prejudice' out of the rack popped it in, sat under her duvet and promptly fell asleep. She woke when the silence told her the film was finished. It took her a few moments to remember where she was and why she was stretched out on her couch covered in a duvet and surrounded by five snoring dogs.

She sat for a moment trying not to remember her dream. Mr Darcy had looked very like Tom and as the dream came back to her she felt angry with him for invading her dreams. Struggling onto her feet she shook off the disturbing image of a handsome Tom on horseback and concentrated on what she had to do.

Dogs were fed in a hurry. Afterwards Ally locked them in their kennels for the night much to their disgust. She was pulling off her boots when the ring of the doorbell was heard. She walked towards it wondering who had come to annoy her this time.

16. A Problem Shared

Yanking open the door, she was greeted by Elaine and the beautiful aroma of chicken potpie.

"My own secret recipe," Elaine told her and looked surprised when Ally groaned.

"What? You don't like chicken? Everybody likes chicken."

"No. I don't like secret recipes in fact I don't like secrets especially ones that relate to a man called Tom. He is the most exasperating man."

Elaine was curious and decided to stay for a while. She removed her coat and made a mug of tea. Minutes later she was sitting opposite Ally listening. She watched while Ally picked at the chicken, eating all the meat and gravy and leaving the veg to one side. Elaine would usually have chastised anyone for doing that. Ally could see she was far too busy ingesting Ally's story. When she finished the whole sorry tale, Elaine remained silent.

Ally watched in frustration as Elaine got up to refill her mug of tea. She sighed dramatically. Elaine ignored her, letting her mind sift through the layers of information to pull out the true facts.

"Come on Elaine you usually have loads of do's and don'ts to dole out never mind all the: if it were me scenarios. What do you think?"

"I think." Elaine paused for dramatic effect. "I think it's incredible that you are talking about something other than racing and flaming dogs. Not wishing to turn this whole thing back on me, but, I do get tired of hearing about poor Luna's this and Butch's that. Now this is really interesting. Fascinating, I'd say. Describe him to me."

"You know what he looks like. He's six foot two, with brown eyes you could get lost in. He has the shoulders of a rugby player, a flashing irritating grin that lingers in your head." Ally paused. Elaine was coughing and raising her eyes to heaven. "What?"

"Ok. I get it. He is a dish, but that is not what I am asking you. I am asking you to land back on earth and tell me what he is like. Does he have any really disgusting points? Does he pick his nose, for example? Is he obnoxious to old ladies?"

Ally smiled at the last comment, she couldn't imagine Tom being obnoxious to anyone. She hadn't considered it. She confessed, "Oh God, I don't know, maybe he does. I have had four encounters with him and he is stuck inside my head."

"Tell me about them." Elaine demanded sitting back in her chair with her long legs stretched out before her. Elaine always had the knack of looking very lazy and relaxed while inside her mind was whirling. She could detect a vast change in Ally. She was sitting upright. Her eyes were sparkling and her voice was changing tone every few minutes. It was clear to her that Ally was attracted to this man. Elaine was dying to meet him and promised herself she would make that happen in the shortest time she could. She wasn't about to let Ally ruin this promising relationship before it got to that first hurdle of being called a relationship.

Ally stopped and frowned. "Hang on I already told you this stuff."

"I know you did. I know it off by heart now. The first time he saw you, you were racing. He talked to your dad but not you. I'm surprised Sam didn't nudge you together. He spent his life on his own. He would have had no desire for you

49

to carry it on as a tradition. Also he, like me, knew your marriage was doomed. The second time Tom saw you. He made sure he met you, at the race where you thoroughly bet him."

Ally sat and remembered that first meeting. "He asked me about the race in Scotland. He wants to enter it. He was checking me out." She sat up straight. "No, not me Luna. He wants her. It makes sense for him to be interested in her." She sniffled and grabbed another hanky.

Elaine was perplexed. "What gave you that idea?"

"Think about it. He is competitive. He has no team. He keeps looking at Luna, I wonder will he offer me money for her. Just let him try." Her hands formed two tight fists.

"No, you are completely bonkers. Whatever spark ignited at your first meeting brought him trundling to your door with the excuse of returning Sam's rig." Elaine saw her friend was beginning to see where this was going. "Then when you went undercover for a while," Ally threw her a dirty look at those words. "He was worried or I am supposing he was and decided to visit to check on you. His solution was to appear with dinner whether he cooked, bought, begged or stole it is not the issue. The point is he is interested in you."

"Or Luna."

The ticking clock was the only sound for a while as both women digested all of this information. The tone of voice was soft but Elaine's words shook Ally, "why did you try to frighten him away by telling him about John. Your past doesn't matter. I think it must have sounded like," Elaine's voice rose - "I will go to a nunnery."

Ally giggled. "Now who is being completely stupid? A nunnery is hard to find." She chewed on her bottom lip. "Besides I heard a rumour."

At Elaine's raised eyebrow, Ally explained about what she had heard at the hairdressers.

Elaine grinned. "I know Luna is great but, wouldn't it be easier for him to just ask you if you would sell her? If all he wants is your dogs then why all the visits and bringing you dinner?"

It was a puzzle, Ally couldn't figure him out.

"If you meet him again, be nice to him Ally. Let it run its course. See where it takes you. Or simply ask him is he interested in your dogs or you?" Her words sent Ally into a fit of laughter, which became a fit of coughing.

Elaine stood up and said, "I am going to go back to my mad house. You are not come in tomorrow. We are in the office so I can manage on my own. Don't take this the wrong way but these days a quiet office is like a heaven sent gift. Too much rowing with Chloe these days is leaving her mother's nerves in a tattered state. A little rest and relaxation at work will be perfect." Elaine busied herself tidying up the dishes. When everything was washed, dried and packed away, she took one look at Ally and said, "Hurry up and get better. I will invite the two of you for Sunday lunch. If he accepts, we can find out a little bit more about him and his intentions. Leave it to detective Elaine."

Planting a kiss on the top of Ally's head she left saying, "relax, go to bed take it easy for the next day or so. I will ring you tomorrow night and see how you are. If you need anything just holler."

Ally promised she would and waved Elaine off feeling much happier than she suspected she should be.

17. Ambitious Planning

Silence is too loud for me she decided setting a hot mug of lemon and honey on the locker beside her bed. With the remote control within reach and a mushy romance novel beside her, Ally was hoping to sleep. It didn't happen. Elaine's conversation stirred up too many unanswered questions. Ally began to list the things she would like to do before she reached forty. She lay propped up by pillows and began to write them on an old envelope.

Number 1. We will win a major race.

She paused and shoved the pen in her mouth, an old habit that used to annoy her teachers. She began to chew thoughtfully on the end of the pen. 'That was easy but it won't happen soon, unless I win the lottery to fund me travelling to a major event.' She added in capital letters; remember to buy lottery ticket on a regular basis.

Chewing on the pen again she considered her next life goal.

'I suppose I would like to have a baby or babies,' she mused thinking of all the fun she and Chloe shared. Then she wrote down, have as many babies as possible. She grimaced, 'you need a man first, and I'm off them.'

She crossed that out. Number two with a huge star beside it was written in fine print across the top and scrawled down the side of the envelope edge. 'Sometime in the next twenty years find a really nice partner.' She considered what nice might mean. 'Elaine was right, it didn't really matter if he was missing all his teeth and had a crooked grin. It was important that he should be thoughtful and kind.' Then she quickly added, 'and he must like dogs, no love them.

Yawning and sniffling she continued to muse on his attributes. He mustn't be lazy but he doesn't have to be out running marathons every week. And, a couch potato will not be tolerated, as it would mean I should have to do all the house work, yard work and bits in between.' Reading it back she grinned because he did sound like Superman.

'No,' she decided, ' money wouldn't come into it. It would be nice if he had a job though he didn't have to be rich. We would have to have the same interests.' She considered this then crossed it out because Elaine and her husband Ben had no interests in common, besides Chloe and each other, and they were married for over fifteen years.

Her eyelids were dropping. She looked at the list with difficulty as the words were blurring into one another. Her last coherent thought before she fell asleep was, 'I don't even know where Tom lives.'

18. Elaine's Loaded Lunch Invitation

Ally was feeling better next day. By early afternoon she was bored with being indoors. She ventured outside for a quick walk in the fields surrounding her house. It was a beautiful afternoon. Early morning rain had cleaned the countryside leaving it enhanced with rich vibrant colours as acknowledged by the tulips bowing heads.

When Ally opened the garden gate the dogs shot off into the field behind the house to search out rabbits and pheasants. Dressed in boots, jeans and heavy layers of tee shirt plus jumper and jacket she felt warm. Her hat covered most of her head leaving only her eyes and nose open to the elements. She was tired by the time she returned to the house. Red faced and with a dripping nose she turned the corner, and bumped straight into the solid chest of Tom.

"Whoa, what are you doing out of bed? I was starting to panic. I called but you didn't answer. Then I saw nobody in the yard, not a mouse to be seen. Now you come stumbling around the corner looking like death warmed up."

"Nice. How kind. You came to deliver insults and?" Ally found it hard to tilt her head back so she concentrated on staring at his neck. "That's an amazing multi-coloured scarf" she told him before remembering what she meant to say, "I am not a baby, am not an invalid. I am a grown responsible single woman. I can cope with a grotty nasty cold. No need for anyone to call out the army or panic."

The blinding colours of his scarf had her riveted to it. "Technicolor" she decided.

"I am aware of how great and responsible you are. I met Elaine outside, she was coming over with a dish of beef stew for you and she decided, I should be the one to stay and scold you for trying to get your death. I left the dish under the empty flower pot at your back door."

"Nice. You and my once best friend are conspiring about me behind my back." Ally snapped back. She ruined the effect by blowing her nose hard into a tissue. She knew Elaine meant well but there was only so much minding Ally could tolerate.

Tom took a step backwards. "You don't look well. I should drive you to the doctors."

Ally wasn't listening to him. John's visit had served to remind her, she was done with bossy, controlling men. She walked around him and with a long low whistle called the dogs to her. "Stop telling me what to do." She rounded on him. "I needed to get out for a few minutes to clear my head."

He opened his mouth and closed it. Walking over to the back door he retrieved the dish of stew. Then handing it to her he said, "You deal with this. I will sort these guys out." He was halfway to their kennels when he remembered he had no idea where to find their food. He turned to Ally saying "sorry you will have to follow me and shout instructions as I work."

Opening her mouth to protest was useless as he was already following Bob across the yard. "Treacherous dog," Ally muttered as Bob led the way to the feed room. Left with no choice she followed clutching the warm dish. She yelled out instructions to Tom in a croaky voice. She had to admit he worked fast despite having a whirlpool of dogs moving around him like sharks. Fifteen minutes later they were finished.

"Anyone ever tell you that you are the most annoying man on earth?" Ally asked.

Tom was shuffling about from foot to foot. "Frequently but luckily, I don't listen. If I had known you were ill yesterday I would have come over. However, I can't stay and help further. I am supposed to be somewhere else."

He glanced at his watch. "Oops by the way I have been offered lunch in Elaine's house on Sunday."

It took a few seconds for the meaning of his words to sink in while she mused on who was waiting for him. He's probably left brunettes behind and moved on to red heads she thought. For some reason the idea annoyed her.

Too much thinking is not good, she decided. Her head was thumping meaning she was in no mood to argue or concentrate. What she craved most was peace and quiet.

"Don't worry about lunch. Elaine hands out invitations left, right and centre. Chances are she will have ten other strangers there." Ally grinned and stared at him, "You might leave with a new friend on your arm. That should make you happy."

"As long as he has a good sense of humour and can cope with smelly feet and snoring, then we will get along okay."

With a shudder Ally said, "Ugh, too much information. You have smelly feet and you snore? And you live at home with mum."

His reply was fast, "Not me, Mac has the smelliest feet and he can snore as loudly as any rock band. You forget, I am every woman's dream."

She smiled. "How could I forget when the whole town is gossiping about your conquests?"

"You shouldn't." He smiled at her and their eyes met. "Are you gossiping about me?"

She felt hot and flustered. She broke eye contact. "I suppose you are going to barge in, demanding a cup of tea." she grumbled.

She stood on the step pulling off her boots against the lip of the step while clutching the stew dish to her. Ally was conscious of his eyes fixed on her.

To her astonishment Tom bent down and smelt her boots.

"Yuck. No thanks. You thought I'm the one with a problem." Straightening up he said, "Remember you have my phone number. If you need anything ring me, but not Friday, I will be away for a while. Take care."

"Somewhere wet and muddy, I hope." She said wondering why he wasn't being more specific as she watched him walk away.

19. Elaine Checks In

Ally ate Elaine's beef stew without tasting it. She found herself dwelling on her latest encounter with Tom. "I hope there is a big black cloud aimed at Tom, or is it possible for you to do that for me?" she asked the jolly weather man on the TV. Her phone rang. She groaned wondering why everyone couldn't leave her alone.

It was Elaine. "I thought you would prefer him to me," was her comment, when Ally scolded Elaine for sending Tom to see her.

Elaine was reluctant to give up on the topic asking, "Any more juicy bits to divulge Ally? Was there a sizzle in the air as you looked into each other's eyes?"

"No." Ally growled down the line. "Absolutely not. Though there might have been if your stew was thrown at him. Thanks, by the way it was really appreciated."

Ally struggled trying to pull the correct question from amongst the tangled mush in her brain and finally said, "I was wondering if you know where he lives as you seem to know everyone in this part of the world?" She paused to cough, "I mean we know about his fan club and harem, but where does he live?"

Without a moment's hesitation Elaine said, "I am sure I can find out for you. Though we both know, you are not presently nor never could be interested in such a suave handsome man even if it is time for you to move on with your life."

Ally didn't have to be sitting with Elaine to know how she was taking this news about Tom. "Stop smiling Elaine. I am curious as to why he is interested in me. I have this persistent feeling he is up to something."

"Ally I will ask you one more thing before I hang up the phone, How can someone as smart as you, be so blind to the obvious. Just accept it. Tom is intrigued. He may even like you or God forbid lust after you. Pity I'm not single or you would have a fight on your hands."

"Need I remind you? Elaine you are a married woman." Ally said.

"Yea, I know you just did. No you don't have to remind me of anything besides I was only saying, that is all. Right, see you tomorrow."

20. Spring Cleaning

Ally was looking forward to summer. This year, she would get the house and garden in tip-top shape. Spring, Ally believed, is the time of year for preparing and mending. She hoped by being busy; Tom, John and the divorce could be pushed to the back of her mind.

Her immediate plan was to paint the wooden fence at the front garden. Rolling up her sleeves she tackled it with enthusiasm. It took two full afternoons of careful constant painting, which was hampered by five eager, inquisitive dogs.

Standing back and admiring her finished work she didn't dwell on the remaining jobs to be tackled. The fence was number one on her long list. The next item was to make the vegetable garden dog proof.

Last year her fruit had come under attack from Bob. His love of strawberries was only surpassed by his determination in getting to them. It didn't matter where Ally planted them because he would open a gate or scale a five-foot fence, to check beneath the dark green leaves. Trouble multiplied, when the other dogs discovered what Bob was at and followed his example.

Her crop of potatoes were dug up a month early, because Luna decided it would be a perfect patch to have a cool nest to keep out of the heat. Butch, Alex and Zoë dug their own burrows in the patch which meant the potato season was over before it had begun. This year she resolved, it would be different she would have home grown potatoes even if it meant erecting a rabbit and dog proof fence.

On Wednesday afternoon she was feeling unsettled. 'Concentrate on the here and now,' she told herself. But she couldn't. Her mind was full of past bad experiences, her marriage and Sam's illness.

She knew if Elaine heard her she would have scolded Ally. Elaine's motto was live each moment as though it is your last. And Elaine did, Ally could vouch for that because she had witnessed many of Elaine's wild moments.

Ally decided to take the dogs for a long walk to the nearest beach, a distance of thirty kilometres away. Families rarely ventured to this stony beach, which made it, hassle free for one adult with five dogs. It was a glorious day. Not a typical Irish Spring day, this was worthy of being a chart buster. The sun was shining. Clouds were absent, the sky so blue Ally couldn't see where the sea began and the sky ended. Five minutes there and she began to relax.

She arrived back home late in the evening. After they had dined, she on a healthy chicken salad, the crew on their usual chicken, potato and vegetable meal, she went out to check her post.

21. John's Letter

Collecting the post, Ally acknowledged, was her first mistake.
She knew, when she recognised his handwriting, it would ruin
her evening. Turning away from the box she considered
leaving it, pretend, she didn't know it was there lying in wait
for her. Instead she took it out.

Opening it was her second mistake. The letter was brief.

Ally,

*I have given consideration to your demand regarding the
house. I have no idea where you got the idea or understand the
reasons why I should even consider paying rent while I am
living in my own house, bought by me, with you, some two
years ago. I have decided the divorce court can decide. In the
meantime I will not be paying rent.*

John

Anger flared at the casual way he could discard her. He
knew she was living on a pittance and would never beg or seek
help elsewhere. He was twisting the knife in with delight. She
grabbed her mobile phone intending to ring him, to give him a
piece of her mind and stopped. It was what he wanted. He had
sent the letter to annoy and irritate her. He succeeded but he
would only discover this if she rang him.

No, she would remain calm and cool. Still it was tough to
hold back. As she yanked open the fridge door the poster for
the northern run caught her eye. She stared at it. 'You are not

going to make the race this year or next year,' her heart sagged as the horrible truth in this statement hit her.

She snatched it off the door and threw it into the bin. Instantly she regretted her rash decision. Ok so it was a dream she couldn't afford. 'Money' Ally thought, 'flaming money is the issue.' She tried not to look at the bills sitting on the table, stacking up, increasing with every passing week. Grabbing a chocolate bar she bit into it and paced about the kitchen, kicking the door shut as she passed. It failed to close only swung back towards her. The wonky kitchen door reminded her she needed to get her house in shape. 'Not only my house, but my life' she spun about and stared outside trying not to dwell on other problems.

When she became Mrs. Allison O'Brien, her biggest problem, in the beginning, was what to cook for dinner. As time went on the problems in her marriage intensified until the day she moved out.

When Sam died, her life changed. She learnt how to cope on her own. She knew it didn't make sense, one woman with five dogs, rambling about a four-bedroom house complete with a huge garden. Chewing on the chocolate bar Ally weighed up her options.

Selling was not a realistic choice, because no one was buying houses. People were renting more, instead of buying their own home. 'Perhaps if I renovate, I could take in a tenant. Make the second story a separate apartment.' Have a paying guest made sense to her. But, in order to renovate she needed money. Ally grimaced. The truth was, if she didn't do something, she would continue to slide into debt.

22. A Rainy Afternoon Clearing Out Clutter

The idea of a tenant danced about in her head, insisting it was a great idea. Ally spent the next afternoon listening to the pitter-patter of raindrops while she cleared out the spare room.

She made three piles, items for recycling, items for re-use and those to be binned. She was beginning to make a noticeable difference when a familiar voice caused her to stop. Listening to the sounds of Elaine, attempting to get in the back door without five dogs traipsing after her, was funny. In the end when the noise became deafening, she went to the rescue.

Pulling open the door she found Elaine standing on the doorstep facing them. Red faced and with her corkscrew hair being blown into her eyes by the draught at the back door she turned to Ally demanding, "How come when I say sit and stay, they merely wag their tails and follow me?" She pleaded, "Please help."

"You know better. It's your tone of voice. When you gently tell them to, sit down please, it sounds as though you are inviting them indoors to party. Instead be firm. Sit." As one unit they sat.

"Stay." She said. They sat in a neat row. Elaine glared at her.

Ally held the door open. Elaine scooted past.

"Thanks. I bring you good news and a pair of rubber gloves because I had my nails done. Chloe is with her Gran, before you ask." Elaine snapped on a very snazzy pair of canary yellow gloves edged with bright orange feathers. "I brought a pair for you. I saw the cleaning experts on the telly wearing them and ordered some, aren't they absolutely amazing?"

"What are these tidings of good cheer or are the gloves it?"

"I learnt a little bit about your new boyfriend."

"He's not my boy friend." She glared at Elaine. "Come on. As you volunteered for this battle, let's get stuck in. Please note my interest in your news is purely out of nosiness."

Elaine looked at the magazines and books piled on the floor. "If I were you, I would hold a sale in the garage."

"Do you think anyone would buy any of these?" Ally held an old car magazine.

"You won't know if you don't try." Looking out into the hallway Elaine asked, "Explain the piles please. And why are we are doing this?"

Ally obliged. Elaine was satisfied. "It makes sense. Let's start.

"They worked in silence until Elaine suddenly sank onto the dusty floor."Enough, I'm exhausted and dusty. How about we have a coffee break?"

Ally stood upright and stretched forward with her arms extended to ease the ache in her back. "I agree time for a coffee break."

23. Plotting and Planning with Cake

Elaine went out to her car. She returned bearing a cake tin with the large fruitcake nestled inside it. "It's a new recipe requiring your opinion."

One bite was enough, Ally smiled, "Bliss. Thank you."

Elaine took a large bite. Her verdict was delivered with a nod, "thought the recipe sounded strange. It has pineapple in it, but, it works. I will put it in my book of favourites."

When Ally relaxed, she told Elaine of John's letter and her angry response. She confessed, "If he appeared here, I would smack him. I can't believe he is so selfish. We agreed way back to rent it, next I discover he has moved his girlfriend in. He expects me to pay half the bills."

"Smacking is too good for him. We should think of a more fitting punishment." Elaine said with enthusiasm. Seeing the dark look on Ally's face she changed the subject. "Are you certain about getting rid of this stuff and the renting idea?"

"Yes I am. I need to do this. It is long overdue and the income generated by a tenant would pay for insulating and updating the rest of this house and help me with the day to day bills."

"Or you could simply move your own dishy lover in, get him to help." Elaine's voice was persuasive.

Putting down her cup Ally said, "Never, ever."

"You can't say ever. You don't know what is around the corner. And Tom is hanging about."

"Don't you think he is too good to be true? I do. Look around you Elaine there aren't too many Bens in this world."

Elaine cut two more slices of cake. Placing one in front of Ally she said, "You can't make a lifelong promise all because of one bad experience."

"Do you want to bet?"

"This is one bet I would love to win."

"You mentioned good news when you arrived. Were the nifty rubber gloves it?"

"No. Helen, the girl who is in a lot of the exercise classes I attend, knows Tom. She went to school with Sarah his younger sister. Helen says, he always has a great looking woman on his arm, is highly competitive and always gets what he wants, woman, and job, whatever."

"We know that. You told me that last week. Now real news would be the solution to the mystery of why he is interested in plain boring old me." Ally's tone was sarcastic. Absently she wondered if Helen was a past conquest of his. She shoved the annoying thought aside.

Elaine paused. Ally waited sensing there was more to come and hoped Elaine wasn't about to cause world war three by saying something crazy.

"This is only rumour. The trouble is it agrees with your crazy idea and so I left it to last. He is supposed to be looking for a dog or couple of dogs to win some big race. The only fact we know is and I beg you to focus on this, he came back to take care of his mum."

Spluttering on a mouthful of tea Ally remembered Tom's casual interest in a lot of things, Luna, tips and lessons from Ally, the Scottish race all of these swirled about in her head. "See I was right, he doesn't want me it's the dogs. He showed a passing interest in the Scottish race to throw me off the scent pretending he was more interested in my lack of finances and he knows Steve."

"Rubbish everyone knows horrible Steve. Remember Tom's mum is ill. He left the high life to come back to this, the sticks to look after her. I can't wait for our lunch get together. We should leave further debate until after the event, agreed?"

"What are we having?" Ally sweetly asked trying not to get into a fight with Elaine over gossip.

"Well, you, I think will be eating your hat and apologising till the cows come home, or, failing that being so sweet that you will make the poor chap sick."

"Bother. I prefer to stick to my original version." At Elaine's raised eyebrows Ally explained, "He is a secret woman hater, exploiting women with a dozen kids of his sprinkled in between. He has no money, wants to move in here, kill me, and sell the house."

"Wouldn't you have fun finding out?" Elaine paused to let that sink into Ally's stubborn head. "First things first, let's go and finish this grotty room. We need to decide on a date for the garage sale. I'll get Ben to make posters with Chloe. She loves colouring. It will keep them busy on Sunday, while we interrogate this kind new handsome friend of yours." With those words hanging in the air she led the way back up the stairs and with a deep sigh waded into the mess before them.

24. An Emotional Encounter

Pleased with the result of turning a cluttered mess into a sunny, blank canvas Ally turned her attention onto the next bedroom. What she hadn't banked on, was the emotional whirlpool that accompanied working on her parent's room. Ally ventured into it every few months to give it a light, quick dusting or hovering. She never lingered.

It was early on Saturday morning. The world outside was asleep. There were sounds of birdsong and the odd car door banging, but she could have been on an island.

"It's not fair," she whispered conceding that missing him was a constant in her life. Her fingers brushed against Sam's favourite jacket. Tears tumbled down her face, washing away all sensible thought. Rushing from the room she dashed down the stairs and out into the yard. She was standing gulping in huge mouthfuls of air, when Tom walked into the yard.

'Why does he always appear when I am a mess?' She wondered. And then all thought was lost in the strange but comforting embrace he gave her. His arms were strong, his jacket smelt faintly of dog and mints. It reminded her of Sam. She burst into a fresh wave of tears.

She could sense his discomfort and was surprised when he merely stood offering his shoulder and comfort. "You must think I'm an idiot, I'm always a mess." She stammered between sniffs wondering why he stood so still. She could feel his heart thumping a sure sign of his distress at having been pushed into such an uncomfortable predicament. Ally was trying to stem the flow. She was aware of the volume of tears seeping through his shirt and jacket.

Pushing her gently away, he pulled a wad of clean tissues from his pocket. "Here, Ally. Lucky for you, I never leave home without them, courtesy of mum and her, in case of, policy."

"What?" She muttered dabbing her eyes willing her heart to slow down. 'I should be kicking him, not embracing him,' she didn't want to dwell on the reasons for the kicking bit. Instead she focused on his words.

"Mums policy - always make sure you leave home with clean underwear on, a pocket full of tissues and some loose change in case you have an accident. We call it her, 'In case of an accident policy.' I have to admit today it is paying off dividends. I never thought it would land me a babe." Stepping further back to avoid the full impact of her swinging arm he said, "Glad to see you appreciate my gesture of friendship and goodwill." He grimaced as he continued to rub his arm.

"I am sorry. I didn't mean to beat you up. Feck. How often have I said sorry to you?" The tingling in her body was fading and her heartbeat was returning to normal. Her suspicions were surfacing. She was no babe. She was a tomboy, always had been and always would be. He might be the enemy who was trying to snatch or buy her beloved Luna from her. At the moment he didn't feel like the enemy. She was struggling to discover what he was.

"It doesn't matter. Friends should help each other, in good and bad times." As he said it her eyes opened wide.

Ally hadn't considered that option. She had considered him a dognapper, womaniser but a friend? No, the idea never entered her head. His eyes, she noted were full of concern.

"Don't you want to vanish into the horizon having seen me as I am - an emotional wreck?" She watched his face.

He squinted and took his time before answering, "Yes, my initial reaction was, run. I mean look at me, how could any woman refuse such a handsome package? I am very big - in the looks department, full of charm and very good at providing hugs. But I've never had that effect on a woman." His eyes

70

twinkled at her. "Seriously, Ally, I agreed to be a friend. I simply was here at the right time to lend you a shoulder, that is all." With a dramatic sigh he added, "I've learnt that is the way it is to be, until the rule is lifted."

She chewed on her lip and worried about being a friend with him. "What if the rule remains a rule?"

"Huh. What are you blind, or stupid? I'll give you five weeks at tops."

Ally glared at him and moved in to punch him once more. "A friend is for life not for five weeks." He neatly sidestepped her swing and she hit clean air.

Clearing his throat he softly asked, "Do I have the right to ask what caused your tears?"

She considered her answer.

"Stop worrying your lip to death. Ally, I can take it, whatever it is."

"I was attempting to clear out Sam's room. I miss him." Ally gave a loud sniffle and found herself enfolded in his arms again. "I'm okay, really I just need to focus on more important stuff, like your mum and my…other stuff." Ally almost said divorce but it might have triggered another wave of tears. Stepping back from him she asked about Tricia.

Tom stared into her eyes. "She is holding her own. She is a feisty woman driven by a desire to help other people. It's the least I could do to come and stay with her."

It was easier for Ally to focus on someone else's needs rather than talk about her stupid roller coaster life, and the trolley load of emotions filling it.

"Sometimes I feel more like a burden to her, as she struggles to put on a brave face for my sake. Sometimes it is good to let it all out." His eyes were twinkling. "I suppose I should explain why I dropped in on you."

"Yes. You should. I am busy." She felt better when they were not being serious.

"Huh. Superman never had to put up with women like you, normally women throw themselves at a sympathetic man who comes to their rescue."

Narrowing her eyes, Ally looked at Tom. He continued. "I came to ask for your help. It's Mac, he loves racing but otherwise Mac cannot see the point in hurrying. The problem being- how do I get him fit? He needs a trainer and so do I. You wouldn't happen to know of a great one, preferably with a team?"

"Are you trainable? Do you take orders well?"

Tom didn't have time to answer, for Ally remembered what was to happen the next day. "Oh. Bother. Tomorrow is Sunday which means we are to lunch at Elaine's."

"That reminds me, I forgot to explain about Mum. Elaine invited her to come with me. But don't worry, you have met her." Ally was staring at him in a perplexed manner as he said, "she and Bob were companions at our one racing event."

"It was your mum." Ally blushed as she remembered the way she behaved.

"Yes, why are you surprised?"

'Not surprised, more horrified,' she thought as memory of their conversation flooded back.

When he raised his eyebrows she explained a little, "I was blowing off steam about Bob begging for food."

Tom felt the need to reassure her. "She probably didn't pass any heed to it because she didn't mention it to me."

Another possible problem popped into Ally's mind. She hoped Elaine warned Ben about inviting guests for lunch. She knew from past experience it was possible Elaine had not mentioned her plans to Ben. She was surprised to hear Tom ask her for advice.

"Ally, how many children does Elaine have? What should I bring?"

When Ally stared up at him she was surprised to see he was genuinely bothered.

"They have one angelic looking daughter, who is the biggest tomboy I have ever met, who loves drawing and football. Ben loves red wine and I have a bottle of his favourite here. I will bring that. Elaine is a chocoholic, so there you go problem sorted."

As he was leaving Tom turned to her and suggested, "How about I pick you up?"

He stepped back, she supposed, in anticipation of another blow to his arm.

"It is a gesture from me, a friend, to allow you to have a drink, if you wish."

Surprised by his kind offer Ally accepted. "Thanks. See you both at one then."

With a wave he was gone leaving Ally to deal with the niggling worry that was tumbling about in the back of her head. How to find out what he was really up to?

25. Tricia

Sunday morning was wet and miserable. Ally dressed appropriately in a large waterproof jacket and matching pants before taking the dogs out for exercise. When she squelched her way back into the yard, she quickly raced through her yard chores. She was in a hurry because though she wasn't looking for a boyfriend, Ally had no wish to meet Tom's mum looking like she had been rolling about in mud. Hoping an hour would be enough time to work a miracle she headed indoors.

Emerging from a long shower Ally stood and considered her face. Not bad, she decided for a person of thirty three who spends most of her life outdoors and whose beauty regime involves soap, water and a dash of sunscreen. Her freckled face was proof to the fact that she didn't always remember the sunscreen. On sudden impulse she pulled a plum coloured dress from a hanger and put it on. The fitted dress suited her slim figure and Ally decided this would be her day of living dangerously. Chloe would not be impressed by her choice, as she considered Ally an honorary aunt and playmate.

Her kitten heel black pumps completed her outfit. Throwing caution to the wind she put on eyeliner and mascara. Glossing her lips with her favourite lipstick, she didn't have any time to reconsider her choices as Tom arrived. He was apologizing before she opened the front door.

"Ally, I am so sorry. We are early. It's not my fault, it's mum." his voice trailed off as he took in the sight of her. He whistled appreciatively.

Ally pulled a face at him and then asked, "Is she ok? You should have rung me. I would have driven to Elaine's."

"No, she is fine. You look good enough to eat. "At her scowl he continued, "but I know you are not on the menu. It's a compliment please take it as it was meant."

Ally smiled. "Thank you. I thought I should make the effort especially as I don't want your mum to think I am a mad woman living at home with a house full of dogs." She glanced at him, "besides a woman has to remember you always dress like James Bond."

Tom jumped forward and suddenly stepped aside, "Sorry Ally this is mum."

Tricia smiled up at her, "Men, they, are all the same. They forget their manners. Hi Ally, I'm Tricia pleased to meet you, again. I'm sorry if I made a bad impression the last occasion we met. I don't normally kidnap dogs but if you get tired of him, I have a home for Bob. I pestered Tom to come over early so I might meet the rest of your gang." She hesitated, "if that is okay with you?"

Ally warmed to the woman immediately. "Course you can, any friend of Bob's is welcome." Glancing up at Tom she continued, "There is one exception. Perhaps you can give me some tips, he simply keeps turning up at the oddest of moments. And does he ever get dirty?" She looked up at Tom and smiled.

"Thanks a bunch Ally. You do know how to make a man feel special."

"We aim to please. Come in Tricia."

As Ally led the way through the house Tricia began to ask questions about the team. Ally was surprised to learn she knew of Sam's exploits and adventures. "He had a fan club. Some of us older women in the village thought he was extremely handsome and charming."

Before they could say anything else they were in the yard. Tricia was in the middle of the five. She simply held out her hands and they walked up to her one by one and nuzzled her palm. Ally held her breath. She felt tears gather. It was the way they used to greet her dad when he was sick. Any other caller would get a bunch of dogs rushing to them but they gently nuzzled her hand and sat beside her. Bob was the first in line, when the others had said hello he was back at her side once again nudging Luna and Butch out of the way. Tricia bent down and hugged him to her.

"Hi Bob, I didn't bring you any treats but I will next time. You are so soft and handsome," she exclaimed. He answered her with a soft huff.

Ally smiled at this.

"And like all handsome men he knows it." Tricia said as she turned to her son and stared at him. "I thought he would never be ready. He took so long in the bathroom I was afraid he had changed sex." She giggled. "Do you remember the time Caroline dressed you up in her party dress with bows in your hair?"

Tom scowled. "I am never to forget it especially as you love telling the tale. I suspect Caroline was coached by her mother."

Tricia exclaimed, "Tom that's an awful accusation to make on your poor sick old mother."

"Nothing poor or old about you," he said."Come on time to go."

Ally insisted she sit in the back of the car saying, "I prefer to criticise from the back seat." The rest of the short drive passed in a pleasant manner.

26. Lunch

Arriving at Elaine's house Tom asked, "Should we wait, we are a little early?" Before anyone else could speak the front door opened and a small tornado hurtled through the door towards them.

"They are here mum; Ally is here with her two new friends." Chloe smiled at Tom when she finished speaking.

"You must be Chloe. I am delighted to meet you," he said bending down and pulling a coin from behind her ear. She raced off shouting with delight.

Tricia gave him a light dig with her elbow. "I told you not to start by showing off. It's the only trick you know. Now she will expect more."

"And who says I haven't dreamt up a few new ones?" He replied with raised eyebrow.

Ben's arrival to the front door ended all further conversation. Ally stepped forward and made the introductions. After welcoming each of them Ben said "you have made quite a first impression on Chloe. I hope you are prepared. She will be attached to you all evening. If she mentions posters and paints I advise you to pretend you don't hear her."

Tom assured Ben he would do his best. They walked into the kitchen where a very calm looking Elaine was basting a huge joint of beef. "Hi," She said, "I hope no one was expecting a five star meal this will be meat, veg and spuds, with a pudding of sorts."

With introductions made the group split up. Ben and Chloe went to set the table. Ally automatically went to join them and was given the cutlery by Chloe to set out. Then Chloe pulled Ally to one side, "Can I sit beside Tom?" she whispered.

"Of course. " Ally smiled over at Tom. He was in for a grilling. She was looking forward to seeing his reaction to the avalanche of questions that were to come his way.

Elaine joined them rubbing her floury hands on her apron. "Tricia, would you like some wine or we have," pausing she looked over at Ben who quickly took the hint.

"We have water sparkling and still, red and white wine, some fruit juices of peculiar colour because someone interfered in the making of them." His eyes were boring into Chloe.

Putting her hands on her hips she said, "I thought they would give it some," she frowned trying to figure out what word was required.

"Style or panache!" Tricia said helpfully.

"I love that word. Panache, panache," Chloe danced about her dad singing it.

He smiled. "Ok. I stand corrected, we have some stylish fruit juice made by yours truly and helped by junior chef to be, Ms Chloe."

"I think without a shadow of doubt I will have to try some of Chloe's delightful drink."

Chloe raced off to, reappearing holding a small glass complete with a colourful cocktail umbrella sitting in it. "What do you think?" She asked, watching as Tricia sipped it.

Licking her lips very slowly, Tricia declared it to be the fruitiest drink she had ever tasted. Clapping her hands with delight Chloe went off again and reappeared with one for Ally and Tom. They both took the drink and without hesitation sipped it. Ally had to give Tricia twelve points out of ten for her acting because it was like drinking lemon juice. "Well done Chloe, it is the most surprising drink I have ever tasted."

While Chloe flipped her attention to Tom, Ally slipped away, still clutching the dreaded drink in her hand. Walking over to Elaine she asked, "What is in it? Should I pour them away? Elaine, will it poison us?"

Leaning into Ally Elaine whispered, "No to all. I had some earlier and look at me. I'm fine. She put some beetroot juice in it but don't worry it wasn't enough to cause a reaction."

Meanwhile with both parents occupied Chloe was taking over. Holding Tom's hand, she pulled him down the hall and invited Tricia to follow them. Tiptoeing down the hall behind them, Ally managed to swap her now, empty glass for Tricia's full one. Then Ally left, grinning as she heard Chloe saying, "Don't worry we have plenty of time to colour some posters before lunch. Mum is always late with everything. Dad said she was even late delivering me."

27. The Cook Plays Cupid

Back in the kitchen the cook waving a wooden spoon scolded Ally. "I have to disagree with you on all counts. He is charming, pleasant and very," Elaine seemed to consider the right word. "Yes he's a hunk."

"Elaine. You are married. Shame on you, it shouldn't be up to, me, your husband to remind you," Ben said plonking a soft kiss to her forehead as he walked past.

"Yes I know, but there is no harm in looking. Is there? I don't mind when other women ogle you. I don't even bat one eyelash." At Ben's surprised look in her direction, Ally nodded her head in confirmation.

He looked from one to the other of them and muttered, "I am never certain if you two are winding me up or taking the proverbial." With both women grinning at him Ben decided enough was enough, and he went to rescue their guests from Chloe's inquisitive line of chatter.

Meanwhile Elaine was pushing her point home. "You make a lovely couple. He is tall, dark and quiet while you are slender and feisty."

Ally interrupted before Elaine married them off and named their children. "Give me a break Elaine. He is here because you manipulated him into agreeing to it. He probably thought it would be a nice break for his mum. Though I'd imagine by now they have changed their minds."

Elaine hissed at her, "Get real. He is here because I mentioned you would be here for lunch. There is no other reason a grown man would come to a stranger's house for lunch." She omitted to tell Ally that Ben had met Tom and was eager to use his business expertise.

Raising an eyebrow Ally ventured a guess, "You think? So a free lunch and not having to do the washing up has nothing to do with it?"

Elaine sighed, "Go and tell them lunch is ready. Please be nice to him during lunch."

"Elaine When have I ever been rude to anyone?"

She looked at Ally and decided not to state the obvious. They both knew that even Ally could lose her temper on occasion. And when she did it wasn't a pretty sight. "Please go and get them."

Ally did what she was told and rounded the others up for lunch.

28. Detective Chloe's Interrogation

They sat around the dinner table while the rain hammered down on the roof but no one noticed. Elaine's roast was declared a success by Tom who was delighted when a giant lemon cheesecake was promised for dessert.

Conversation was flowing until Chloe, well coached by her mum, began to ask Tom a string of pertinent questions. Though Ally quickly surmised Chloe put her own twist on the questions.

Chloe began with the simple ones. "Where do you live Tom? Do you live close to Ally?"

He explained simply by saying he was living with his mum. His answer was accompanied by a quick light smile, which vanished as soon as he heard her next question.

"Is that because you hate house work stuff or because your girlfriend kicked you out?" The question was asked as Chloe played with her vegetables.

Ally choked on her meat and was shot a look by Elaine. Tom merely sat and stared at Chloe with his mouth open.

Chloe calmly doled out a dollop of ketchup onto her plate before stating, "On the telly they kick him out when the man is a mess or if he is horrible and nasty." She squinted up at him. "And the nasty ones are the ones who seem to be the nicest."

Tricia was the first to recover. "Chloe, I will tell you Tom's worst secret. He is the world's most untidy man."

"How do you know that is his worst or biggest secret? There is a boy at school who was always very nice to us. Then one day all our crayons went missing. They spilled out of his bag when I accidentally kicked it over."

"What does that teach you, Chloe?" Ben tried to change the topic.

"Always be honest or as Granddad Mick says, if you are not you will always land in a whole pile of shit."

Elaine interrupted, "Right, anyone for more beef?" When everyone shook their heads she said, "Chloe would you like some more."

Chloe was not one to be pushed off a topic so easily. With a toss of her head she kept her attention on Tom as she asked, "do you have a girlfriend at the moment or a wife? What age are you?"

Tom shook his head in an attempt to delay his answer. He had no wish to find himself staring at another tricky question, which would land him in more trouble. "I am not married but I have to say I have never met such an interesting girl as you Chloe. Perhaps you should be in the police force."

Chloe grinned then said, "If you don't ask questions then you never find stuff out. Dad tells me lots of stuff that turns out to be rubbish. Imagine this, I asked him to explain a sperm bank to me. His answer was: it is a bank where sperm are kept safe and sound." With a shake of her head, she said "He takes a lot of shortcuts in his answers but I am lucky because I know how to use the internet. So I ask the computer questions and it tells me all I want to know."

"I spend a lot of time on the internet finding out different stuff as well," Tricia decided Tom needed rescuing.

"Like what?" Chloe tilted her head and considered what the answer might be.

"Like how to bake the best chocolate biscuits in the world." Tricia smiled at Chloe as she spoke.

Ally noticed Tom sitting back and looking a little annoyed. She wondered if Chloe was right about him. He never volunteered information. She wondered what he was hiding. She decided she should ask him more about himself. With difficulty she focused on the conversation.

"Gosh I never thought of using it for stuff like that, I usually ask mum. You should ask yours."

"Good idea Chloe, but sadly my mum died long ago." Tricia said.

"So did Ally's mum. Perhaps they are hanging out together. They could be swapping recipes and knitting woolly hats and jumpers for angels as they don't seem to wear a lot in any of the pictures I have seen." Chloe frowned at Ben. "Stop laughing dad. It is possible, you know because none of us knows for definite what happens when you die and go either up there, or down there."

"We are not laughing at your idea Chloe. I'm laughing because it's great. How about helping me tidy up these plates and stacking them on the drainer then we can have dessert or tea or coffee. Or would you rather paint?" Ben asked.

In answer Chloe looked at Tom, "Would you mind if I did some painting by myself? I ate a lot and I'll have my dessert later."

"Of course I wouldn't mind. I am looking forward to eating your mum's cheesecake. If it is anything like her dinner it will be marvellous." Leaning down he asked, "is it the best cheese cake in the world?"

"Oh yes. You will love it or there is something wrong with you if you don't." Chloe skipped off to her room.

29. Race Day Date is Set

The atmosphere lightened when Chloe left.

"She is a good kid but always asking questions. I apologise Tom." Ben said.

Tricia answered first. "Gosh such an inquisitive child, Tom used to drive me mad with his questions mainly because they were so technical minded and our brains don't run the same way. That was his excuse as he stormed off to his best friend's house, where apparently they were amazing and knew the answers to all his tricky questions."

Tom grimaced. "Yes, however, I should point out that Mark and his family were mechanics, of one kind or another, even his mum was a computer technician." His eyes dropped to the table as he sighed. "In ours there was always knitting, sewing and make up lying around. It's a wonder I ended up as straight as I am."

The twinkle in Ally's eyes alerted Tom. "And yes, before these two treacherous women beside me say it," his smile lingered on Ally.

Elaine winked at Ben. He shook his head and smiled. He knew his wife was matchmaking. Until today, her efforts had been wasted. This time he hoped she was right, because every now and then he caught a glimpse of tension between Tom and Ally. He hoped for Elaine's sake, she was reading it correctly. Ally was like a sister, he wished to see her happy.

Tom explained, "I was used as a mannequin so it didn't matter if I was wearing a dress." Laughter bounced about the table as he continued, "I will state for the record for this court, I never wore make-up."

His mother inclined her head and opened her mouth but he silenced her with a wave of his hand. "No. Wearing face paints at Halloween does not count, does it Ben?"

"Most definitely not, or wearing make-up when you wake because your wife and daughter think it would be funny to use you as a model while you are sleeping."

Elaine coughed, "I hate to interrupt this male bonding session. There is cream or ice cream to accompany the cheesecake."

Ally put a dollop of cream on her plate and sighed, "I love coming here for lunch. Chloe's inquisition is worth putting up with because the food is great. I would go as far as saying: the risk of heart burn due to over eating is worth it for the chance of having dinner here. Thanks Elaine."

Tom joined in giving his own thanks for saving them both from a day of his disastrous cooking.

Tricia explained further, "my hands have been giving me trouble, part of the chemotherapy I suppose. They tingle so much sometimes that it is hard to pick up a plate or cup. So cooking is not my forte these days."

With Chloe safely occupied the conversation became more varied, they all discovered they had many likes and dislikes in common. It came as no surprise that everyone loved dogs but Ally was shocked to hear the others hated cold temperatures and snow filled landscapes.

Elaine was a little more tactful than her daughter as she asked Tom, "Where do you work, Tom?"

Clearing his throat in an apologetic manner he began with, "I literally play with money for my living."

"I think I said this to you the other day but it must be tough in this economic climate "Ben said.

Tom shook his head, "No, very boring work really."

"He was doing great until the bankers messed us all up. Now Tom is working on his own but he will make a success of it, he always does." Ally noted the note of pride in Tricia's voice and wondered what happened to his company.

"Yes I have known better days but I got off light in comparison to many. So with no workforce, I am lucky in that I can choose my own working hours. Working from home means I am on hand if needed. Though, sometimes I have to travel to meet with investors and clients."

Tricia smiled. "Yes, he is a workaholic preferring city life and working. He brings his lap top everywhere with him especially now…" Tricia glanced at him and paused, "When work is so hard to find."

Ally tucked these pieces of the puzzle that were Tom away in her mind. She supposed she was another distraction while he was stuck in the boring quiet countryside.

Everyone could see how uncomfortable Tom was feeling. Tricia feeling sorry for her son, as he had been the starter, main course and now dessert smiled at him and said, "I'm an awful nuisance of a mother."

Leaning across he took her hand. "Rubbish, I am enjoying being with you."

Ally watched them together. Whatever else he was, he was good to his mum. Another brownie point, she didn't dwell on it. They were only friends. She understood how important his family was to him. She guessed he would not spend his life alone. He probably hoped for a future complete with a wife and as many children as time allowed them to have.

Tricia glanced at Ally, "there is something I want to ask you two."

Tom frowned, "whatever could that be?"

"When are you going to hold this race? I have heard so much about your dogs and now having met them I insist I am there to watch it."

Elaine sat up straight. "What race?" Her eyes were shining as she rubbed her hands together. "Great. I'll be starter."

Tricia laughed, "I'll be referee."

Ally felt as though she had been pushed into a box, there was no way out. She gritted her teeth and said as pleasantly as she could, "the date and time were not decided on."

"Well, let's do it now." Elaine left the table and returned with a calendar. Ally groaned. She was beaten and she knew it.

"How about Easter week? Perfect, Ally, there will be no school work for us in case you come to blows. Chloe can come and watch, what do you think Tom?"

All eyes swivelled to Tom. "It is up to Ally. She is the boss."

Elaine smiled. "Deal done. The race is set for 6th of April. Ouch."

"Sorry Elaine." Ally hoped her shin was throbbing. She didn't like being backed into a corner. The conversation reverted to more mundane events.

When Ben steered the conversation onto financial investment the two men became engrossed in their conversation leaving the women free to gossip about the village.

By three thirty Tricia was having difficulty keeping her eyes open. Tom suggested they should go and she was reluctant to agree. An hour later they were on their way home.

30. A Feather Light Kiss

Tricia fell asleep in the warm car. Taking a quick glance at her sleeping form, Tom suggested to Ally he take his mum home first. She agreed.

Ally was feeling relaxed. Her anger over the race evaporated as she remembered Chloe's rapidly fired questions. Besides, she was curious to see where he lived. When they turned into the driveway she was surprised to discover the house was one she often admired when she drove past. The detached house was sitting on a beautifully landscaped site. Ally's exclamations of wonder and delight brought a groan from Tom.

"Wait till you see the improvements Mac has made to the back garden."

Ally was prepared to see a repeat of the pristine daffodil laden front garden. The words died on her lips as she spotted the six foot high fence and the potholed lawn beyond the house.

"To keep Mac in, I presume?" Ally questioned. "Does it work?"

Tom grinned. "Sometimes but Mum lets him wander at will through the house and the back garden. I created an elaborate fencing system that allows him access to the back."

"I see." Ally got out of the car. Looking around she saw Mac sitting on top of a children's slide. The moment he spotted them, Mac slid down and bounded up to the fence. To her surprise he shot his paw through and pulled open the first gate. The second gate had a bolt, top and bottom.

Smiling she told Tom "I am beginning to appreciate the size of the problem you have. She asked, "Can I go in to him? Where are the others?"

"Of course. Watch out for, you know what, I haven't had time to scoop anything today. Borrow Tricia's welly boots, they are here by the back door." He blushed. "As for the others well, I, I borrowed them."

Before Ally could reprimand him for misleading her or find out more, Tricia woke and Tom helped her indoors.

Mac was nudging Ally's pockets. She looked at him and muttered, "Bribery doesn't happen in my house, just good old fashioned play with your favourite toy as a reward for good behaviour." When she moved away, he trotted alongside with his tail waving back and forth.

Ally looked at the house and saw Tom and Tricia in the conservatory. He appeared to be fussing about Tricia, tucking a blanket around her and handing her a glass of water.

When Tom joined them outside he stopped and stared in amazement. Mac was jumping a series of three make shift jumps. Ally had found some logs and buckets for the support of her fences. Broom handles and canes from the garden served as the cross poles. Mac was sitting expectantly at the end of the first jump. Ally using her no nonsense tone of voice said, "Stay."

Mac lifted his tail off the ground looked at her and remained where he was. Ally took two paces backwards. With a loud woof, to show his impatience Mac sat and stared at her. When Ally stepped back beside him and shouted "Go," he ran alongside her, jumping over the fences as they came to them. With a loud shout of delight she bent and gave him a hug.

Tom turned to her. "Thanks. I never thought of that, it's a good way of exercising him."

Sitting on an upturned crate they had a very serious discussion about Mac's good points and in particular his defects, which, were beginning to mount up. The air temperature dropped dramatically but neither of them noticed it. Tom was only conscious of how nice this was sitting here with her.

Ally wondered if he was always this inattentive to women. He seemed to be struggling to focus on what she was saying to him. She brought the topic, which was puzzling her out into the open, "you play with money for a living?"

"Yes. I can count."

She wondered why he sounded defensive and attempted to put him at ease so she could find out what were his true motives. With a sigh she said, "A mysterious man of many talents." An irrational thought popped into her head, if she wasn't married and if Tom was a little less handsome then perhaps she would not be troubled by the knowledge of his huge fan club.

Turning to face her he stared into her grey eyes."Not mysterious at all or talented you should talk to my sisters. They would have a list a mile long about my weaknesses." He smiled.

Ally squinted at him trying to guess what he thought of her and why he was sitting here with her instead of dating one of his adoring fans. Their eyes locked. Her heart beat raced making the moment stretch on. She couldn't take her eyes off his, until she saw him leaning forward. Too late she realised his intentions and she couldn't avoid the tender fleeting kiss he planted on her lips.

'Heaven' she thought then recoiled in horror at the very recognition of having such a treacherous thought. A little devil in her heart was saying this was proof he wanted more than friendship.

Her reaction was immediate, every nerve in her body tingled as she jumped away from him as though stung "Why did you do that?" her voice was harsh.

He asked a question of his own. "Do you not feel the connection between us?"

She scowled. Tom seemed pleased. He began to rub the dog's head saying "I'd best feed you before checking on mum.

Ally, give me a minute or two and I will drive you back home." He left her sitting there. She was scowling. He set off to feed Mac with a huge beaming smile on his face.

Ally didn't hesitate the moment he was gone she stood up and left. She didn't think of anything bar putting as much distance between them as possible.

31. A Wet Muddy End

Ally wasn't stewing; she was steaming as she marched home. Having decided walking the two miles by road might involve a meeting with Tom, she had taken a short cut through the fields.

'How dare he?' The question was dancing, tumbling in her head, as quickly as her feet hit the ground. She didn't notice the muck or wet grass, because of her anger. 'Was it a dare? I am a fool. He has taken me for a fool. Yet he could be right. I am an idiot. How stupid is it, to go out to lunch with him, especially as he sees me as a challenge.' She faltered mid step another suspicion entering her mind. 'I'm an idiot. Did I not say one thing and then he misread my intentions. I shouldn't have gone to the stupid lunch with them. What a mess.'

She trudged along the path at the edge of the field silently repeating, 'I will forget him. I will never speak to him again. I will stay out of his way. I will avoid him. We will never meet again. It can be done. Though I only live a few fields away, I have to remember, we had never met until recently.' It became a strange and weird mantra but by the time she marched back into her own yard she was almost convinced.

Her conviction lasted until she finished feeding and looking after the dogs. "What I need is a drink. Terrific he is driving me to drink!"She murmured bending to tousle Luna's coat. Luna promptly planted a wet tongue on Ally's cheek.

This simple act led her to think of the kiss. Tender, but promising so much more, she decided as the image of his brown eyes swam before her.

She decided she was an idiot. He didn't have a racing team. He was play acting at it. She didn't want to get mixed up in another relationship based on incorrect feelings. Once is enough to fall into a trap like that.

Yet, a tiny niggling voice was insisting, she had it wrong. With a sigh she banished all stupid musings, headed for the welcome warmth of the house. Ally removed her coat and got as far as pulling off one Wellington boot when she stopped and looked down at her feet. "Ah no," she groaned realising the boots were not hers but Tricia's.

Biting her bottom lip she considered her options. She needed to collect her shoes but had no desire to meet him. If Tricia found them questions would be asked. Ally didn't want anyone knowing of her stupidity.

Ally debated if she could drive back and collect them before he noticed the shoes. That way, she might avoid meeting him for a few days. They were, after all, sitting outside the back door. She could simply sneak in and swap them. Ally's delight faltered when she remembered she had consumed almost a full bottle of wine. Anger flowed through her veins as she remembered how easy it was for him to kiss her. She supposed that was why he had claimed a kiss. Her anger peaked because in her mind, preying on a slightly inebriated woman was not playing fair.

'Well stuff you mate, I will walk back and leave them on the doorstep. Collect my own shoes and walk back. I won't have to see anyone and nobody will know I was there.'

Having locked up the house Ally set off, this time, clutching Tricia's warm boots under one arm encased in a plastic bag. It was a perfect evening for a walk. The air was crisp, the sky filled with twinkling stars. Ally looked upwards and stumbled into a pothole, the water dribbled into her wellington boot. It was cold. Squelching along in muddy, wet boots increased her misery.

"So much for the twinkling stars," she muttered. She tried to forget, how her treacherous heart had responded to his kiss.

At that precise moment her phone rang.

"Lo," she growled into it.

"Excuse me, I must have dialled the wrong number. I was looking for a highly sought after lady by the name of Ally to discuss the latest findings on the dish she brought to lunch."

Ally grimaced. She could tell, by Elaine's tone of voice, she was smiling.

"Elaine I am wet, tired and slightly wobbly after the ample glasses of wine Ben poured into me. What I do not need right now is a dissection on how great your cooking was and as for points scored I would say Chloe twenty, you, twenty five, Ben thirty for filling me up to the neck with wine and that odious giant nil, nada."

Elaine knew better than to ask what the matter was. She patiently sat down beside Ben, stretched her feet out and waited. She had counted to five when Ally began, "It couldn't have gotten any worse than it did. But it did because, he kissed me."

Elaine grinned. "Great. How was it on the Richter scale of fabulous, nine, ten or a mere one hundred out of ten?"

"Zero. I didn't want it to happen. But." Ally was beginning to calm down.

"It did." Elaine calmly finished for her. "How did it happen? Was it a long sensuous moment, a tender fleeting kiss full of promise and hope? Or a big dipper?"

Despite her wet foot, wobbly head and cold hands Ally grinned. "What the hell is a big dipper? Are you living on a different planet than me? Elaine stop smiling. I can hear you smiling and this isn't funny."

"I am smiling because I am delighted you are getting some full blooded male action at long last. Where are you now? You sound as though you are sloshing about in the river."

"Close." Ally gritted her teeth and yanked her foot out of another pothole full of water. "I am on a covert mission to retrieve my shoes and give him back his mum's wellingtons."

"Oh, I think I see."

Ally let Elaine's wild imagination run riot for a few steps. "Elaine stop putting two and two together and coming up with fifty five. I have to go I am almost there."

"Okay this sounds much more interesting than watching the talent show on the telly. I will meet you at the laneway below his house in ten minutes. I can drive you safely back home. And on the way you can give me the full techno-colour version no skipping bits or points will be deducted." With that she ended the call.

32. The Return Journey

The night sky was a black curtain. The friendly twinkling stars had vanished behind thick clouds, having decided they no longer needed to watch an idiot Irishwoman splashing about in a field.

The lights were on in Tricia's house. For a moment, Ally paused to admire it. 'Dam it', she thought 'why are they and everything about them so nice? Why am I doing this? I should have given the boots to Elaine. She would have taken them with enthusiasm to Tricia for a full version on the Ally and Tom saga.'

That thought stopped her in her tracks. 'There is no Ally and Tom anything,' she decided putting her right foot forward straight into the muddiest deepest puddle in the field. Ally tried pulling her foot out but it was stuck. When she finally yanked it out it, she did it with such viciousness she was sent zipping backwards landing on her bottom. "Ouch." She sat there for a minute to catch her breath. The effort of getting to her feet left her hands in a mucky state. Her hair felt heavy. Raising her hand to her head, she discovered her hair was wet and muddy. The rest of the journey was accomplished with the speed of a snail.

Arriving at the house Ally let out a low whistle at the hedge and when no Mac came charging for her, she deemed it safe to proceed. What she didn't bank on was Tom putting out the bags of rubbish at the precise moment she tiptoed through the hedge.

She knew from the way he looked at her, he was trying not to pass comment on her bedraggled appearance. "Lost? Or simply hiking?" he ventured as he walked over and pulled a bramble from her hair.

She scowled and indicated the boots. He took them, walked to the back door where her shoes sat. Dropping the boots to the ground he retrieved her shoes, retraced his steps and handed them to her. His eyes were fixed on her face. Those same eyes, she couldn't fail to notice, were not twinkling they were radiating giant fireworks of amusement.

"Thank you for a lovely day, and please thank your mum for me." She said graciously while trying not to shiver with cold.

"Why don't you come in and ahem, clean up and thank her yourself?"

"No, I must get back home." Ally flicked her wet hair from her face.

Tom asked, "Would you like me to drive you?"

"No thank you. You have done enough for me." Ally scowled as she heard the words leave her mouth. She sounded like a prim schoolteacher from a nineteen forty film.

"I could do a little more." With raised eyebrows he smiled at her and winked.

"No thank you." She was now mad at herself for risking this meeting.

She recognised the teasing tone in his voice as he said, "I appreciate you coming back to see me because I too am curious about our kiss. Okay, let's put it to the test." Before she could move a muscle or yell at him, his left hand shot about her waist and bending his head to her they dipped and kissed. In the dark recess of her mind she heard a clunk and knew it was her shoes falling onto the path.

The kiss was even better than the last one, full of hope and heart thumping insinuation of more to follow. The tenderness was her undoing as she leant into him and responded. All the electrons in her body jumped, scattered and she was helpless, caught. Her senses were darting about, knocking all logical thought from her mind. Taking a breath she smelt his cologne and identified the faint whiff of Mac. His skin was warm to the touch and suddenly it was hard to breath. Somewhere dimly in the back of what used to be her mind, she recognized that she was melting in the arms of the enemy. 'Worse,' she thought, 'I am in a big dipper!'

Tom had intended to drop another whisper of a kiss on her lips, but he found it wasn't enough. He wanted more. He had a need to taste her, to explore every inch of her being. He couldn't get enough and he didn't want it to end. She looked fragile but he was learning she wasn't.

"Tom, your phone is ringing where are you?" Tricia's voice was faint, worried.

Tom released his hold on Ally. She slipped out of his embrace.

Bending down she retrieved her shoes. Tricia was standing at the back door shouting for Tom. Ally panicked darting into the shadows. She stood there feeling like a teenager hiding from a parent. Tom followed. Leaning forward he whispered, "Same place and time tomorrow?"

Ally turned, marched away hissing, "Not in this lifetime buddy. Get a hearing aid."

She had arrived angry and fighting, she was leaving feeling as though her world had turned on its head. Walking on the grass verge, Ally kept to the shadows and darted out his gateway just as Elaine arrived in her car.

33. No hugs allowed

Elaine's car hiccupped rather than purred as it moved alongside Ally. Elaine noted she was marching along arms swinging shoulders straight wearing a don't mess with me expression. Elaine let the passenger window down, "I don't think I should give you a lift Ally, you are covered in muck. Fancy walking home?"

Ally bent down, yanked open the door and jumped inside, saying, "Drive, fast. Don't say another word till I have showered and had a mug of coffee along with a large brownie with a side order of a large tub of ice cream."

Elaine hid her grin as best she could and stuck to Ally's request. Walking into Ally's house she turned on the TV. Ally headed for a shower. Twenty minutes later she came into the kitchen looking tired and sad. Elaine handed a mug of steaming coffee to Ally, placed two giant muffins between them before sitting in the armchair close to Ally. She waited in silence.

Clutching the mug to her chest Ally said, "Please just talk rubbish. I, the world's greatest idiot, feel like crying."

Elaine leant forward. With a toss of her head Ally told her, "No hugs please. I need some normality."

"Ok. Wait till I tell you this little gem from your godchild. I collected her from school today. Chloe handed a note to me. It was from the principal Mrs. Molloy. Chloe related a story to everyone. Unfortunately it was in her grandfather's exact words." Clearing her throat, Elaine began "Molly said to Daisy."

"Hang on who are they?"

Patiently Elaine explained, "Molly the sheep, is the mum and Daisy- her baby lamb."

"Life might be easier if your daughter, my goddaughter were interested in dolls."

Elaine continued with her narration, "Molly said to Daisy, - Daisy, I'm really pissed off feeding you, go try the bottle Mick has. So Daisy did and now Molly is happy because she doesn't have to keep feeding Daisy, but, Mick is hopping mad because he has to do it."

They collapsed, laughing like two teenagers. When she could speak Ally summed up the problem, "the cursing phase continues."

"Yes. I have to go to the principal's office because this story was related during a break. Half the school is using pissed off with dramatic effect."

"I'd love to be a fly on the wall for that conversation." Ally said feeling a lot better.

34. Past Loves Remembered

"Good, you are looking more relaxed, take a deep breath and tell me about your encounter of a mucky kind. Leave nothing out." Elaine held scooped up her brownie and bit into it.

As Ally watched Elaine settled into the deep cushioned settee, sipping on the hot drink.

"Get the gleam out of your eye. There is nothing going on between us. Ever. And I mean ever, full stop. All of my past relationships have been messy horrible mistakes culminating in my grand finale, my wedding."

Tilting her head to one side, Elaine considered the last statement. "Ah, not all of them. There was that nice blond haired guy. What was his name?" Elaine scrunched up her eyes as she tried to work out who he was. "All I remember was every girl in the school dreamt about him. You were the lucky one to bring him to your debs. You dated him that summer."

Ally flinched as the whole sorry tale came flooding back to her. "Yes Alan was nice. He was too nice for me and any girl. He later moved to New York with his boyfriend. See the one guy we all thought was okay, was okay but not for us." Shaking her head she looked at Elaine saying, "But you, on the other hand, always dated the butch guys."

Elaine agreed with a nod, "Yes. They terrified my dad, reminding him of a younger version of him. So, he, in turn terrified all of them except for Ben who was never terrified by anyone especially dad." Elaine smiled, "Because dad was coaching the rugby squad and Ben was his star player. He would have climbed Mount Everest on his hands and knees to keep Ben happy."

For a few minutes they sat companionably in silence both remembering a time when life was simpler. Elaine was relieved Ally was no longer upset. However Ally's thoughts were simmering. She was puzzled over the complete mess she was making of everything.

35. Advice is Given

Ally tightened the belt on her dressing gown, "Well as I keep saying you don't have to waste a second worrying about me and men." She frowned at Elaine. "I mean what I say."

This statement lacked conviction. Elaine leant forward asking, "Are you nuts? He is crazy about you. Ben noticed it. And you know how unobservant he is about affairs of the heart, including our own."

Ally tilted her head to one side and considered this unusual statement. Ben never passed comment about anyone. "Why, what did he say? Not that I am interested."

"It wasn't a lot, but enough for him to let me know he witnessed a spark of chemistry flying about our dining table. I hope Chloe didn't notice it. She is old enough in her ways without becoming a romantic at the tender age of nine." Elaine continued on in a hurry, "And yes before you ask, I too noticed. He follows your every move. And you are too dumb to acknowledge a good thing when you see it."

"Are you trying to pawn me off? I wish I had been more alert to notice the amount of drink I consumed, courtesy of Ben, which is probably why the first you know what happened, never mind the second."

"What happened?" Elaine sat upright her eyes open wide.

"Nothing. I can't be interested in any man because I am married, in the eyes of the church, the law and mine, to John."

"Oh. Him? Never mind John, Ally. Tom is much more interesting. What happened when you returned the boots? You were pretty worked up as you ran out of his driveway." She grinned then said, "you were moving like your ass was on fire."

Taking a deep breath Ally said, "I was in a state of shock because, he did it again."

Elaine's smiled widened as realisation of what 'it' was, "no. How dare he show his true feelings by giving you another kiss? The cheek of him." Her smile faded when she looked at Ally's face.

"It wasn't a simple peck on the cheek. It was one of those funny one's, you know the Fred and Ginger move." Realising she was digging a deeper hole for herself Ally stopped.

Elaine jumped up from her seat, and sat beside Ally. "Wow. How many women of our age would love to experience one of those babies? Was it horrible? By that I mean stupendous and romantic to every other woman on the planet yet horrendous to you alone?"

Despite herself Ally felt compelled to be truthful. She let her mind and body take her back to that moment. When he pulled her closer she had been like putty in his hands, powerless to stop it. She could recall so much, his cologne, his warm skin, his strength pouring through her even though the kiss was tender and soft. She acknowledged for the second time the tenderness was her undoing. Sitting here with Elaine, the memory of it had the power to pull the breath from her body.

Biting on her lower lip and squishing up her eyes she considered speaking truthfully. If she ever needed help it was now. She needed someone to understand her dilemma and be a friend no matter what decision she made.

"It was beyond exquisite, if I am truthful. He is tender and kind. It trickles and leaks from every pore of his body so much so that you want to cling to him forever. But, Elaine." The tears began to roll down her cheeks.

Elaine was silenced by this unusual display of emotion and listened as Ally continued to explain. "I know it was the stuff of movies. The moment every woman searches for when you feel a deep connection with another being and you never want it to end. But I am not free. Worse I have so much baggage inside of me making me an emotional train wreck. How could any relationship survive a journey with me? I know divorce is right, yet for me it feels like another death. I grieve for it while I am angered by memories of it. Worse, I doubt everything I do."

Elaine's raised eyebrows had Ally nodding. "Yes, everything even racing. I doubt my ability to compete, every single time I line up at the start of a race. I am not like you."

Elaine opened her mouth to speak but decided against it.

"I don't feel confident and brave. I tremble and quiver. How could I have a relationship when I am such a mess? I'm not normal. Look at the way John has recovered from our break-up. He has bounced back complete with gorgeous girlfriend. He didn't even pause for breath before he was out on the road testing new models."

At the mention of John's name Elaine had to speak. "Let's not talk about him. He thrives on pushing people around, she's young and gullible, she will learn."

Ally thought about that for a moment, "As I was when we met. He assumed he could manipulate me. I rebelled but too late for our relationship, I should have been honest from the beginning."

Elaine spoke softly, "Okay. I agree Tom is not John. If I were you and Tom appears at your doorstep in the next day or two be happy. You have been honest with him. He knows you are competitive, he knows you are animal, in particular, dog crackers. He also has discovered the funny brash side of you when you are tiddly and decide to do the impossible all by yourself, for example trekking across the fields at night to secretly return a pair of boots. In short he knows you are nuts and if the man comes traipsing back to you I advise you to take hand and all from him. Look at it from his point of view."

"I am and still I don't know. Elaine. I cannot ask anyone to hang about for two years. Besides by then everything could change. He could move away and be working in London or New York, even made his millions, be living in the Caribbean with an exotic zumba dancer."

"Oh Ally!" She was smiling, "what am I going to do with you? Happiness is within an arms grasp for you."

Ally realised she had been the reason why so many things had gone wrong in her life. She was determined this time she wasn't going to make the same mistakes. She tried to figure it out, "I think I have never really taken my time with a relationship and next time I will take it so slow it will ache. But I have to sort out so much with John, the house and all that stuff before I can truly consider a life with anyone. No, Tom is not for me, look at the Luna thing. I need someone honest."

With a deep sigh Elaine stood up and stretched. "Okay but promise me if you get upset over John, the divorce, anything at all, you won't bottle it up, you will come to me and talk."

Ally smiled. It was an easy promise to make. They talked some more about the plan for the next day and Elaine left feeling a little happier because she suspected that Tom was just as stubborn as Ally.

36. Tom

Tom walked around the next morning in a daze. He had no idea what to do next. He didn't intend to kiss her it simply happened. It was obvious to him, they were meant for each other, but how could he convince her? Next problem rattling around in his head was: he needed to deal with the Steve issue. He dialled the number and waited.

Steve answered as warmly as ever, "good the deal is done, how much do I owe you and when can I pick her up?"

"There is no deal done and there won't be." Tom said but before he could utter another word Steve's words hit their mark.

"Well looks as though you won't be getting your hands on that nice little contract in Cork, hurry up I can't wait for ever." The call ended.

Tom groaned, and redialled the number. The number rang out. He knew Steve was making a statement and waiting to see if Tom would take the bait. However, it had the opposite effect on Tom. He no longer wanted to have any contact with Steve. Next on his list was how to tell Ally the truth and make her understand it was a business deal made long before he met her.

Funny how everything can change in a heartbeat, Tom mused. Now he had no intention of taking Luna away from her. He wanted to help Ally, be there for her but how to convince her of this?

When he confessed he liked Ally to Tricia on Sunday evening, she revealed she liked Ally on sight. Tricia summed

Ally up as no nonsense woman who cared deeply for people and left the trivial commercial side of life where it belonged: on a shelf. Her words put a huge smile on Tom's face. He agreed and knew after watching Ally with Chloe, Ben and Elaine he sensed these three people were the closest thing to family Ally had. Later that night his mood had darkened and she wondered what had happened. But when she pressed him more on the topic he clammed up.

When Tricia spotted him putting the cereal in the fridge the next morning, she pretended not to notice. She knew enough about her son to know sooner or later he would seek advice.

At five thirty Tricia decided she could stand it no longer. Tom was sitting in the conservatory pretending to read the newspaper. He was reading it upside down. With a smile she said, "I have never seen another person do that."

"Sorry, do what?" Tom pulled himself out of his daydream and back to the present.

"You are reading the paper upside-down. I believe you haven't read one column in the last half hour." Smiling at him she flicked a piece of lint from her cardigan "That was a lovely meal yesterday. I should ring Elaine or better still, go see her and thank her in person. But I am too tired I wonder if you would go."

Tom agreed. "Of course, I should have thought of doing it."

"Perhaps you could check on Ally too." Tricia was surprised when he dropped back into his chair again.

"Hmm I don't know. I sort of spoilt my chances there by taking the lady by the shoulders and kissing her."

Colour flushed her cheeks, Tricia leant forward, "Really? You didn't tell me this last night. How did you feel after she stormed off?"

Tom narrowed his eyes and looked at her. "How on earth would you know that? Were you spying on me, us?"

Tricia shook her head. "No, I wasn't. It's an age old story. What else would a woman do when a handsome man shows how he feels so quickly? She is only getting to know you and then you move the goal post. Some women don't like being surprised." Tom opened his mouth and closed it when his mum raised her index finger saying, "don't listen to what Caroline says. I, and you, know if the same thing happened to her she would knock his block off."

Tom agreed with this clever summing up of the whole situation including the Caroline scenario. "But what do I do next?"

"It depends on two factors. What she feels and what she wants."

Tom narrowed his eyes, "don't my feelings come into this?"

"In a fashion yes." Tricia smiled and the smile reached her eyes. "Don't forget, you have one advantage, me."

Tricia got up. Walking over to Tom, she hugged him to her. "You have to think up a plan of action to convince Ally, you are serious and you are not your dad or her ex husband. You are a mature man who knows what he wants and usually gets it. But it is highly probable that she is simply not ready to trust another. How patient can you be?"

Tom thought of their lingering kiss. No other woman had made him feel that way. No one had come close to her. He wanted her forever. When he looked over at Tricia he was not smiling, "As long as it takes. For now I will join in the pro Ally group by going over to Elaine's house to help Chloe with posters."

37. Colouring and Confidence

Chloe was delighted to see Tom and his large packet of markers and crayons. He frowned at her whoop of delight when he appeared. He was relieved to discover the excitement was due to the arrival of Fred. Chloe took hold of his hand and dragged Tom indoors. "Say hello to Fred."

The pup was weaving at his feet. Tom solemnly said, "Hello Fred, how do you do?"

Chloe led the way towards the kitchen. "Ally says she will help me to train Fred. It's great you came because I have too much to do." With a dramatic sigh she pointed at the posters on the table, "Dad says the more of these I colour in, the better it will be for Ally."

Frowning down at her Tom asked, "I don't understand what this has to do with Ally? Aren't the posters for a school fundraiser?"

Elaine was folding laundry in the kitchen. She remained silent with difficulty. She had promised Ally she wouldn't encourage Tom to call on her. But if Chloe said anything then it wouldn't count. Elaine smiled as she heard Chloe say, "No, this is for the sale at Ally's house."

As he was unloading his collection onto the table Chloe continued, "she is selling all the cr..," a flying tea towel landed on Chloe's head. She stopped for a moment."Sorry mum. Tom, she is selling rubbish from her house. Dad says she has an awful lot of rubbish to sell."

Tom glanced at Elaine who explained further, "Chloe is right. There is to be a garage sale featuring all of the extra bits from Ally's house. You must have noticed the boxes of books, her dad never threw out or got rid of along with a wardrobe, lockers, and lamps all carefully stacked and waiting for re sale. Are you getting the picture?"

"Yes. This is happening, because she is thinking of letting half the house. Am I right? I overheard her conversation with Ben on Sunday."

At her nod, Tom wondered if he should go and offer help to get stuff ready for the sale. Elaine seemed to guess what he was thinking, "Ben is going over with us tonight and we will see what we can do to help. The sale is next Saturday if you have nothing better on I know she would appreciate all the support she can get."

Elaine left them to their colouring in to finish her hovering. When she returned to the room an hour later Tom was diligently sitting at the table colouring. There was no sign of Chloe or Fred. With a toss of her hair, Elaine muttered, "typical where is she now?"

"Fred needed to go out so…they did."

"And she left you to do the donkey work for her." Elaine picket up a marker and began to colour the large outlined letters on the A3 page.

"For her and for Ally, mostly for Ally." Tom confessed.

Elaine was finding it hard not to interfere but if he asked for her opinion she would give it honestly. Elaine believed they deserved all the help they could get in finding and holding onto each other.

They worked in silence for a few minutes. Tom was figuring out how much he could ask Elaine, "Mum thinks I need to step back give her time and work on my subtle plan of attack."

Without looking up at him Elaine smiled, "I like your mum and the way she thinks."

Tom lifted the crayon from the page. Looked over at Elaine and considered her for a moment. Blushing he said, "I know you are Ally's best friend. I hate to ask you to keep a secret but can I tell you something?"

At Elaine's nod Tom simply said, "I love her."

"I know."

He looked astonished. "You do?"

Laughing at him Elaine said, "Course I do as does your mum, Chloe and even Ben. I would add Ally but she is so bogged down in her past failures she is afraid of ruining your life. I think you need to give her time, and be patient with her. I agree, a plan would be good, but a soft gentle plan of action. You can't go storming in like an action hero," she frowned. "No, you need to be more old school think Cary Grant, Katherine Hepburn. In fact there is something you could do, she loves those old movies but can't find them on DVD. Ally is hopeless about ordering stuff on the internet and never goes shopping."

Tom considered this. An idea was taking shape. "What else does she like?"

They worked on the posters while trying to figure out ways of breaking through Ally's lack of self esteem. The banging of the back door announced their boss and Fred had returned. "Mum I hope you didn't go over the lines. " Chloe said picking up one of Elaine's abandoned sheets.

"Course I didn't. Who taught you to be the world's greatest colour inner?"

"Dad." Her reply was delivered with a killer grin. Chloe considered Tom's work. "Not bad, you forgot to put your name on the bottom like a real artist."

Tom smiled. "I'll take some home. I'll leave them back tomorrow evening. Is that okay?"

With the plan agreed they parted company. Tom drove home knowing he should leave Ally to make the next outward move but that didn't mean he should be lazy. He decided he could not tell anyone of the reason for his initial interest in her, her team and in particular Luna.

38. Selling and Bonus Points

The bright posters in the village shops attracted a lot of attention. A small crowd gathered in Ally's garage at eleven o'clock on Saturday morning. Elaine and Ben were manning a stall and Chloe was handing out paper cups of orange juice to those who stood around talking. Chloe pointed out her mum's homemade biscuits to everyone explaining, they would be a thank you bonus present to anyone who bought something.

Tricia appeared at mid-day with two younger versions of herself. Caroline who was the eldest was dark haired and tall like Tom. Sarah was blonde and smaller, but reminded Ally of Tom in the way she moved her hands as she spoke. Everything reminds me of him, she thought with a groan and turned back to answer a question about a table lamp. Tricia had also brought along two of her grandsons.

The twins, with twenty two years of sporting enthusiasm between them, immediately ran to the sports equipment on a makeshift table and said, "Wow." Owen and Robert sat either side of the table and worked their way through it.

Tricia spent some time in conversation with a group of women and Elaine noted when they left they took half the contents of the garage with them. She also saw Tom's sisters bought various bits and pieces. But when she looked over at Ally she frowned. She did not look happy. Elaine moved closer to her.

"What's up?"

"I have this strange feeling someone has engineered the whole day on me." Ally tucked her hair behind her ears. "And there is the worrying rumour about Tom. Well I think it was about him. It sounded like him so it must be him."

Elaine frowned. "You are not making sense please explain it to me."

Ally remembered the conversation she overheard in the hairdressers. With gritted teeth she said, "The one about him having his heart set on buying one of Ally's dogs."

"Gossip like that you shouldn't listen to, you know that. Besides it has nothing to do with today. The sale is going great. There is a constant flow of people in and out of here."

Ally looked around her. She didn't know most of the people who were in her garage. "These people know him or Tricia. I feel…I don't want to become the local charity case. Besides we know Tom's interest is in Luna only."

"No. I don't agree. Fact one, you are selling off stuff that is in good working order and people have bought what they need. What is wrong with that? Fact two, have you asked him outright about Luna? Why not? I'll tell you because you know it is untrue. Seriously Ally, you need to relax. Look at Ben. I haven't seen him make this much conversation since our wedding day and there was a compulsive order on speaking to everyone that day."

Attempting a smile Ally sighed, "Yes you're right I am becoming paranoid. I must relax a bit more."

She gave it her best shot and began to talk to people as they came and went. By three thirty they were all tired and hungry. The crowd had dwindled to a few. Ally looked at the makeshift cash box. It was bulging with coins and notes. "I think I've exceeded all of my hopes on this one. Thank you all very much. Chloe and I ordered pizza, for the lot of us. It should be here in a half an hour or so. Let's close up shop, tidy up and go and eat."

39. A Surprise

Chloe bounded into the kitchen first. She came to an abrupt stop saying, "Oops, look at that."

"Look at what?" Elaine asked. She stopped so fast Ben and Ally collided with her. They stood mouths open and looked about the kitchen. On the table sat two boxes with notes attached to them. Ally read the first note, "I thought you might be tired. Sorry I couldn't be around to help you, Tom."

The second note was more mysterious, 'please open later.' Ally groaned and sank into the nearest seat. "See I told you, manipulated and stalked."

Ben looked from his wife to Ally and said, "I have no idea what you are talking about but I for one appreciate any gesture associated with feeding us. Please, lay this spread out." Elaine carried the second box upstairs to the bedroom before Ally got a chance to dump it in the bin.

While Chloe went to check on Fred who was being minded by Bob, Ben laid the contents of the box on the table. Elaine and Ally set cutlery on the table. The ringing doorbell announced the arrival of the pizza. Ally went out to pay for it. She returned saying, "I forgot the pizza and how are we going to eat this?"

Ben simply said, "With great delight, thank you very much."

She sat down and looked at the spread before her. There was a collection of salads, a roast chicken and a huge soft loaf of bread. A large bottle of minerals bore the label, for the attention of Chloe and a small bone for Fred. But sitting in the centre of the table was a giant chocolate fondant cake.

They gave it their best but there was loads of food left when they eventually declared not another mouthful could be eaten by anyone of them. Chloe was looking sleepy. Elaine suggested Chloe and Ben take the dogs for a walk while Ally and Elaine tidied up the remains of the feast.

Ally knew there was enough food to feed at least three more guests. "Please take most of this home Elaine I will never finish it and it would be a shame to let it go to waste." Ally said as she divided the food into plastic containers.

"It was kind of him." As she spoke she could see Ally tensing. Elaine tried again. "Well at least you didn't have to face him and be reminded of the other night. But it shows he thinks of you and cares, doesn't it?"

Despite the overwhelming feeling of tiredness Ally was still capable of thinking. "One kind gesture doesn't constitute commitment merely take it as it was meant - a kind gesture."

"Good, I thought you might explode when you saw it and take it straight back to him."

"It would be a long drive, Tricia said he had business to attend to in Cork. I suspect she put this together." Ally said, feeling better.

"Don't forget the second box please tell us what is in it tomorrow." Elaine said as the noisy arrival of Ben and Chloe with Fred dancing about them ended their conversation. A short time later Ally was alone.

More tired than she thought possible Ally headed for her bathroom to take a much needed relaxing bath to help forget all about Tom and kind gestures.

40. A Thoughtful Gift

It didn't work because on walking into her bedroom she saw the box on her bed. Ally walked around it. She was cautious but suspected she was overreacting. 'It might as well be a bomb the way I'm treating it,' she decided.

Her suspicions that Tricia had sent it encouraged her to open the box. When she did she grinned. The old black and white films were her favourites; Cary Grant and Katherine Hepburn's "Bringing up Baby" was playing within a short space of time. It worked its magic and Ally fell asleep.

Her dream shook her, Cary Grant had turned into Tom and she was the impish leading lady. The story changed until it became so mixed up with her life that Ally woke in a daze not knowing who she was or where she was.

She pushed the dream to the back of her mind and began her morning routine. 'A dream is merely the sign of a tired brain and body. I can forget all about him." However this proved to be easier said, than done. For each time she opened the fridge door, the bits of left over food reminded her of him. On the second occasion she opened it to get milk and found herself staring at the remains of the chicken. She considered feeding it to the dogs. Ally supposed it would be a petty thing to do given, there wasn't enough to feed one, so she would only start a fight amongst them.

Counting the proceeds of the sale Ally was surprised and elated. She had enough money to pay off her electricity bill and buy some paint for the rooms she was about to decorate. It wasn't a fortune but it was a huge step in the right direction.

Ally thoughts turned to the northern run. It would remain a wishful dream but there is always next year. She stared at the poster saying, "next year I will take part."

The one other thing she wished she could do was park her feelings for Tom for the next two years. To accomplish this Ally would have to stay out of his way. She knew this would be impossible. The reason was simple for tomorrow was Race Day.

41. Race Day

Ally felt a shiver of excitement run through her. A race was a race and every race counted to her. She suspected this was going to be a tough race. She rang Tom to confirm the rules of the race.

They had already agreed on two dogs pulling their rigs.

Tom was feeling confident. He tried to rattle her confidence saying, "My practice runs have been improving. We should give you a good race. Let the games begin, see you at two o clock."

"Ok. See you later, and Tom, you should wear your lucky racing shoes."

His parting shot was, "who says we need luck? Besides they are shorts not shoes."

When Elaine appeared she was not on her own. "I thought Chloe and the moron dog might like to watch." She indicated Fred who was tugging at the door mat and Chloe who was smiling at him.

Ally watched them for a moment. It had been her idea for Chloe to have the puppy. When Ally saw him, on the television show, her heart melted. He was a tiny, furry bundle who would grow to be a giant husky. She knew Elaine and Ben had been searching for a way to help Chloe learn a little responsibility and keep her occupied. Running to find her phone Ally soon made her case for the pup. As Chloe was a true outdoors person from the moment she could walk this seemed the ideal solution. Ever since the pup arrived Chloe had been the model of a perfect child.

"Mum we are not watching, we are going to race." Chloe hands on hips followed her mum into Ally's kitchen. The pup dropped the mat and raced after Chloe.

"Watch this Ally, watch." Chloe said, "Fred Sit!" The pup stopped his circling and tilted his head sideways causing one huge ear to fall over one eye. Chloe gave an exasperated sigh, then repeated her command. Fred obliged. Chloe swooped on him showering him with hugs and kisses.

Standing upwards she asked, "Can we race, please? See how good he is. He is only little so we should start before you."

Ally considered the safer options. "We could use a helper. We will need to find you a flag."

"I have made a few." Chloe ran off to collect her flag. Ally turned her attention to the serious business: the race.

The course they were going to take was a simple one, with only one twisty nasty double bend on it. The path was wide and not a favourite one for walkers. Ally hoped this meant that no spectator would be knocked over like skittles in a bowling alley.

Chloe appeared minutes later with the wheelbarrow and Fred sitting in it. The barrow contained some homemade signs. She began her explanation before she reached her mum, "Dad helped me to make these. " The signs were made from cardboard stuck to old bamboo sticks. She read aloud, "Danger mad humans and dogs racing ahead: Race time 2.30 pm."

Ally grimaced. "Wait till I catch up with him, mad my foot. There is nothing mad or crazy about us."

They were a noisy group as they made their way to the river where a small group appeared to be waiting for them. Elaine confessed, "Word might have gone round, but it is a small village."

There was no sign of Tom. Ally wondered if he had decided against racing. However noisy barking from Luna, announced the arrival of Tom, Tricia, Mac and Toby.

Tricia wondered aloud at the number of people gathered around them. "Elaine told a few people," Ally explained.

"Are we placing bets?" one elderly gentleman asked another.

The second man grinned and took a euro out of his pocket. "Ok. My money is on Ally, she is half cracked, like her old man. She will win."

A younger lady pushing a buggy was smiling at Tom who politely smiled back at her. Ally tried hard not to notice this exchange but wondered if there was anyone he couldn't charm.

The dogs were getting impatient. Ally suggested they start. Luna took a look at Mac and turned away. Ally noticed this and smiled muttering, "Good girl. Let's show him our tails."

Tom heard this and made a great show of talking to Mac. "Don't listen to her Mac you are number one team. She can't hurt our feelings."

Chloe shouted over to them, "Ally, are you going to ever start?"

Her words brought a murmur of approval from the spectators.

42. Ready, Steady, Splash!

Standing on a fallen tree trunk Elaine yelled, "On your marks, go"

Caught off balance by the sudden start Tom was thrown backwards and had to jump back on to his rig. Both teams lurched off, bicycle tyres of the rigs rattling along at an even pace. The dogs were howling. Their tails were wagging. Tom was doing his best to remember the racing tips he had picked up. With hedges and spectators becoming a blur his sole thought was, "I need to win."

But to his surprise he managed to stick by her side encouraged on by the spectators lining the route. He knew his team were tiring but he encouraged them to race on and they kept pace with Ally's pair of dogs, Luna and Butch, until the long curving bend with the gentle river flowing beside it.

Ally shouted at them, "Gentle, whoa. Gentle." Her team slowed down.

Tom was concentrating on the fact he appeared to be gaining on her. Eyes straight ahead, Tom didn't consider any reaction to his actions. Now, he thought shouting at Mac to race on. The dog obliged and for a mere second Tom believed they were going to leave her far behind.

His feeling of elation lasted for two wobbling seconds. As the rig began to tip over he shifted his weight to one side and closed his eyes hoping he had acted quickly enough. He hadn't, the rig became unbalanced as the dogs increased their pace around the bend. One second more and it became apparent that though the dogs could cope with the bend at such a speed, Tom and his rig couldn't.

The rig turned the corner and tipped onto one wheel. It happened in slow motion as Tom found himself flying through the air, with everything about him becoming one hazy loud blur until he met the dark water.

The loud splash was accompanied by an appreciative roar from the crowd. Tom was embraced by the dark freezing water and his clothes were pulling him under.

'What an embarrassing way to die,' was his only thought as he fought his way towards the surface.

43. Superwoman to the Rescue

Ally heard the shouts of horror, followed by the loud splash. She pulled her team up. Jumping from her rig she ran back along the path to the river bank. Her heart was pounding. She shivered hoping she wouldn't have to dive in, though it was April and sunny she knew the water was ice cold.

She couldn't see him. Her eyes scanned the dark water as she continued to run along the bank. Then she saw him splashing and spluttering in the river. His fancy new jacket was weighing him down. The water was sucking him under. She didn't think as she dived into the river. Ice cold water left her gasping for air. Threading water she glanced back at the bank hoping for instructions as to which direction she should go.

Then she heard Elaine shouting, "head for three o'clock Ally."

She obeyed, pushing her head down and flipping her feet with all her might. Ally came up for a breath. A shudder of relief coursed through her, she was close. He was floundering about in the water, fighting to swim towards the bank but the strong current was making it a losing battle. Ally stopped beside him. She could tell he wasn't happy to see her.

"Are you crazy? What the hell did you jump in here for?"

"I'll just swim back then shall I?" Ally retorted. Her teeth were chattering. "Here, take this jacket off you." She struggled to help him remove it but eventually they got it off.

"This dam current is too strong." Tom was cursing his stupidity; swimming had never been one of his strong points. He preferred having his feet firmly fixed on the ground.

His teeth were chattering. They were beginning to sound like a background track on a rap song. He was losing the battle to stay calm.

To his surprise she smiled saying, "don't fight it. Go with the flow."

When Tom shook his head in denial and attempted to swim upriver again, she shouted out, "Watch this, scaredy cat!"

Turning her body downriver Ally let the current pull her along, as Tom watched he saw Ally being driven towards the bank one hundred meters further along from where he had made his spectacular entrance. Elaine and the spectators were standing on the bank. She was holding what looked like a pole.

He saw Ally being pulled from the river by Elaine. His spirits flagging he followed her lead.

'I'm crazy,' he decided. Being tugged along by the current was an un-nerving sensation. Suddenly the pole was inches from his face, he grabbed it missed and continued to search for it when suddenly it hit against his shoulder.

"Sorry Tom." Elaine yelled.

But it didn't matter he had managed to grab on to it with his left hand. It appeared to be an eternity before he scrabbled to the bank. Elaine and Ally grabbed hold of him to help him clamber out just as the small crowd surged forward to help. Sitting on the warm grass Tom wondered if this was a new low for him, being upstaged by a woman.

Ally was showered with praise. "I forgot you swim like a fish Ally." The woman with the child in the buggy was saying.

"Talk about superwoman, I should collect twice, once for you winning the race and the second time for saving the day but he should score points for such a spectacular dive." The elderly gents moved away to discuss the finer details of the bet.

Chloe and Fred ran over to Tom. "Here, I'll get Mac and Toby, you mind Fred." Tom remained where he was and did what he was told. He had counted on winning the race, to help him in his plan to win her heart. 'All is lost' he thought. 'Best suck it in and pick up the pieces.'

Ally walked over to join him. "Okay?" She asked.

"If you consider embarrassed, smelly and cold okay, then I am great." She was looking pretty good to him, despite the white face, blue tinge to her lips and wearing a coat of mud.

Standing up with difficulty, he said, "thanks to you, I am alive, so everything is better than okay." His eyes were glued to hers and as she looked at him everything changed. It was a subtle flicker but the moment stretched making it feel like they were alone but they weren't or he would have warmed them both with a kiss. The moment passed when Fred nudged his knee and dropped a chewed stick at his feet.

"Thanks Fred, just what I need another smelly stick. I suppose we should get cleaned up."

Tricia joined them, patting his arm lightly she didn't make a comment. She knew how competitive he was and how hard this must hurt. Beaten again by a woman and worse humiliated this time.

"Oooh Tom it was an awesome sauce dive." Chloe giggled. Hugging Mac, she said "Don't look sad Mac, it wasn't your fault, was it Tom?"

It was her words and the hug that followed that lifted him out of his misery. He looked from her to his two dogs. They wore sad and miserable expressions. He noticed the women were focused on anything but him.

Ally said, "now we know everyone is alright I'd better go find my team and bring them back home. If anyone needs to shower, change or fuel up in my house just follow us."

Tom tousled the top of Chloe's hair, "You are right Chloe. It wasn't Mac's fault. I was stupid. Come on, do you want to ride on the rig or the barrow?"

Her answer was a fast whoop of delight as she scooped up Fred and hopped into the barrow. Tom cold, tired and hungry headed back for home. Elaine obliged by steering his rig.

Chloe was making plans, "we will have to get you in better racing shape Tom. Your driving skills were stinking. You were pulling and yanking on those poor doggies' heads. They were mad to go faster but you weren't letting them. And then at the bend you were supposed to go slower." She suggested he get some serious training done before his next race.

With a smile he stopped walking long enough to pull a packet of wine gums from his pocket. "Here you go Chloe they are a little soggy but have your name written all over them. I think you deserve them for all your hard work. "

As they continued on Tom was soon brought up to speed with all the news about the horrors of raising a pup called Fred. Elaine interrupted to suggest he take Ally up on her offer of a hot shower and some tea but Tom, to her surprise, refused the offer saying, "I'd best get the dogs and mum home. I'll need a change of clothes anyway. But thank you, everyone."

"For what?"

"For not rubbing my nose in it." He said. "Tell Ally not to worry I have the lawn mowing list and I will not renege on my bet." After saying goodbye to Chloe, Elaine and Fred he left quietly.

44. Elaine gets Sneaky

For the next two weeks, life was not easy for Ally or Elaine.

Ben became ill with the man flu. Elaine spent her days trying hard not to moan about his failure to deal with a heavy cold.

Ally's plumbing had gone on strike. A local plumber called Pete, who was tall, blonde and handsome, was fixing the problem for her. However, while fixing one problem he discovered many others. Her pipes and plumbing were in dire need of some love and attention. This news didn't improve her humour. After a long discussion with Pete, it was decided to put off any further improvements until Ally could afford it.

Elaine sought refuge with Ally one afternoon when Ben declared he was going to watch his entire collection of Clint Eastwood western films.

Chloe, Elaine confessed, was shipped off to her granny's house to indulge their mutual love of baking biscuits. With a basketful of ingredients and a strong reminder about not cursing in front of her grandmother Elaine dropped a kiss on her head and left.

What Elaine omitted was the detailed conversation she had with Caroline in the baker's shop. Ally took one look at the cake box Elaine carried and smiled. She was sanding down the walls, taking the last bits of paper from them before she began the task of painting the room.

"Hi Elaine, thanks for coming over to help. Coffee now or later?"

"Later. Because I have a feeling if I have one of these now I won't start work."

It didn't take long to set up their table, brushes and rollers and within minutes they were painting.

It was a pleasant day. The windows were open wide to allow the paint fumes to leave as quickly as possible. The radio was blaring loudly as they worked. Conversation was non-existent until they stopped for a coffee break. The snoozing dogs and chocolate filled women enjoyed the peaceful afternoon.

Ally was watching Elaine.

Having been interrogated previously about Pete she suspected Elaine was plotting something with the very handsome plumber in mind. She hated to burst Elaine's bubble of enthusiasm but Ally knew it would be safer to do it sooner rather than later. "It won't work you know Elaine."

Elaine's heart jumped. "What won't work?"

"You trying to fix me up with Pete. He is not my type, or any woman's." It wasn't often she got to pre-empt Elaine and when she did, she enjoyed doing so.

"Shame." Elaine said, while thinking, 'but Tom doesn't know that.'

After a moment she looked at Ally. "How did you find out? About Pete, I mean."

"It didn't take long to suss out. He has great taste, loves shopping and need I say more?" Ally was smiling and humming away to herself, believing that Pete's sexual preferences would sort any of Elaine's matchmaking hopes for a long time.

With a groan Elaine announced, "I am sorry I have to leave now but I have to go to the Parent Teacher meeting, the proper one this time, which I hope won't be as bad as meeting her teacher to hear a specific complaint."

Elaine paused to ask, "Ally, as you are Chloe's godmother. Would you like to step in?"

"No, I am sorry. You are on your own." She steeled herself not to cave in as she usually did. Ally said, "I will not face those teachers and listen to all the complaints and reasoning as to why Chloe does what she does. No Elaine. I am sorry but I couldn't do that no matter what you promised me."

"Well it was worth a try. See you tomorrow, if I survive." With a dramatic sigh, Elaine left Ally to get on with her painting.

45. Tricked into a Date

Ally learnt from Elaine of the ladies in the village delight at Tom's kind offer to mow their lawns. He, rumour had it, was suffering greatly from aches and pains resulting from mowing so many lawns.

The ringing of Ally's mobile phone interrupted Elaine's account of the story. Ally's heart began to beat faster when she heard Tom's voice.

"Ally, Owen and Robert told me about Mac's success in agility work. Thank you for giving them your time and attention. "

Ally smiled at the sound of his voice. She had wondered after the wet ending if he would hide from her for a long time. She tried to ignore the irrational flip her stomach did. Elaine, she noted, had not moved discretely away as was her habit when the phone call was of a personal nature. Instead Elaine sat with a huge grin on her face.

"It is Elaine you should thank. She was there one afternoon when Mac dragged Robert into the yard. She persuaded Robert to bring Mac to me. I didn't do much. The two boys did the hard work."

"Robert told me you are working wonders on your house. I've been thinking of you, often, as I mow lawns." His voice was cool.

"I am trying. It is a long process but the new radiators and boiler should make a difference. Pete is being a great help."

"Glad to hear it."

She wondered why he sounded annoyed. She supposed it was because he didn't like the sound of Pete being so helpful. Ally decided to leave him guessing about Pete. "Yes, Pete is great. He arrives early and works till way after dark."

The only response she got was a tight, "hmmm." She smiled and waited.

"Well there is something I need to talk to you about. Besides I need a break from Caroline, she has decided since my dive into the river that I am accident prone. She is driving me nuts."

'Good,' Ally thought, 'glad something is irritating you because you've been constantly annoying me.' Before she could say yes or no she heard Tom say he would pick her up at eight and they might as well get something to eat along the way. She was left standing with her phone to her ear as he hung up.

"Nice" she muttered. "Talk about taking it for granted."

"Who is taking who for granted?" Elaine enquired.

"Don't play the innocent you know Tom was on the phone." Ally rounded on her. "What did Caroline tell Tom about Pete?" She stood watching her friend squirm under the intense stare and waited for an answer."More to the point, what did you tell Caroline when you last talked to her?"

Elaine admitted defeat saying, "Must have been someone else who told her about Pete. Honestly I didn't ring her up and say, guess what Caroline? Ally is entertaining a dishy plumber in her house at all hours."

Ally relented. "I know you didn't. It was Robert." Frowning she confessed, "It's getting worse, Tom has assumed I am going out with Tom - tonight. Perhaps I should be out when he arrives. What do you think?"

"Or maybe you should advantage of the offer of a free dinner and some adult conversation."

"I don't know about the conversation bit, what have we got in common?"

Giving a deep sigh Elaine told her, "Ally. Take a chance and go out. You might enjoy it and if you don't, call me. I will come and pick you up."

Panic entered Ally's eyes. Elaine noticed, and asked, "What's up?"

"Where is he bringing me and what the hell do I wear?"

Smiling lightly Elaine said "trust me, you have loads to wear all hanging in my wardrobe. Come over now. I will sort you out."

"But you are taller than me." Ally almost wailed. She hated the thought of a date which she had never agreed to, and stepping out of her normal routine was not comforting.

With a raise of her eyebrows Elaine said, "So what? You are forever giving out to me because I wear short dresses, or as you call them long tops. If they are short on me, they will be perfect on you. Come on no better time than now. Chloe will enjoy this, I hope."

46. Dressing Up

One hour and many dresses later Chloe, wearing her mum's highest pair of stilettos plus a very trendy pair of sunglasses, was trying on hats of various sizes and shapes.

Turning to her mum she asked, "Has Ally not made her mind up yet? I told her the nicest one was the blue one." Sighing dramatically Chloe sank onto the double bed and petted Fred who was sitting on a pillow chewing on an old trainer belonging to Ben. Then she clambered up and began to bounce as though she was on a trampoline.

"Shoes off." Elaine said.

Chloe obliged kicking them high into the air announcing, "My friend, Leona has a huge trampoline." Then she continued on bouncing until Fred bounced onto the floor. Chloe promptly abandoned her bouncing to sit on the floor fussing over Fred.

Ally confessed, "I have no idea what to wear. You have so many, please help."

Winking at Chloe, Elaine said, "the blue one. You have all the accessories for it, you can wear your dishy navy blue kitten heel shoes. They are gathering dust in your wardrobe. I will be over at seven and will apply a light.." Elaine narrowed her eyes, "and I mean light sprinkling of make-up and you will be ready for the ball."

Shaking her head Ally told her, "there is no need to go that far, I wouldn't feel comfortable. I need to feel as comfortable and relaxed for the battle I suspect is going to take place."

Chloe stopped bouncing and looked from one to the other of the grownups, "What battle? I thought a date was a nice thing. Isn't it?"

Elaine laughed at her, "it is for everyone else but Ally has not been on one in a long time and that," putting her fingers to her lips she continued, "it is top secret."

"It's not top secret. Everyone knows Ally stays home and minds the dogs."

Ally's heart sank at those words. It wasn't the implication of her being a spinster at home tending her dogs it was far worse than that. It was the manner it was stated as though it were a fact. An awful chill took hold of her. She had a premonition of a disaster about to happen.

47. Inspection Time

By six o'clock Ally was ready, moisturised and perfumed enough for a sultan. To make sure there was no eau de dog on her person, Ally was very generous with the spray.

She was fussing with her hair when she heard racing feet and excited barking. Elaine breezed into the room with a cheery smile. "I thought you might make use of this, I forgot all about it." Ally gasped when she turned around, Elaine held a very smart jacket in exactly the same shade of blue as the dress. Elaine, she noted, had pinned a conquer cancer pink ribbon to the lapel of the jacket but for once she let the comment go. It should be taken in the spirit it had been made in, besides it was a nice gesture.

"Ally, are you ready can I come in?" Chloe ran into the room followed by Luna and Fred each of them carrying a sock in their mouth.

"Sit," commanded Elaine. Fred and Luna, to everyone's surprise, sat. The socks were taken from them with difficulty. A deep huff announced the arrival of Bob. He marched up to Ally with his nose high in the air. "Who let you in?" She asked staring at Luna whose latest trick was opening doors. Bob gave her legs a light lick and sat looking up at her.

"He likes your legs." Chloe giggled.

Ally smiled, she felt a little better knowing everyone, Bob included, approved of her dress.

The sound of a car pulling up on the gravel driveway had Elaine glancing at her wristwatch.

"Tom is early. I'll go stall him. Come on Chloe time for us to make some idle chit chat."

48. A Dreamy Location

When Ally entered the kitchen conversation stopped. Tom jumped to his feet. Though his smile was warm she could tell he was nervous from the way he kept fidgeting with his hands, pushing them through his hair and glancing at her then Elaine. She supposed his agenda for a successful night might read like a recipe, pick up date (usually gorgeous), take her to romantic restaurant, have light conversation with a lot of flattery sprinkled on top, finishing with the lucky lady and Tom spending the night together.

Elaine took charge saying, "Right let's go Chloe. We have a lot of energetic dog sitting to do from the looks of it before we can lock this gang up for the night. Maybe you could brush Luna."

"We will have to catch her first." Chloe said with a giggle.

Elaine grinned at Ally, "You look great, both of you, but what are you waiting for, scram."

Tom took the hint and opened the door for Ally saying, "Yes dare I risk saying it, you look beautiful Ally."

Ally glanced at him and decided to take the compliment lightly. "Thank you. You don't look so bad yourself. Will I drive or will you?"

"No, I am driving. We will do this by the book."

She couldn't resist teasing him. "Whose book?"

"Mum's. She loved to remind us about old fashioned manners and etiquette saying they should never be forgotten."

Curiosity made her ask, "Okay so where are we going?"

"Your carriage awaits you. And it is a surprise."

When they were in his car and heading out of town Ally said, "I stupidly assumed we were going to eat in the hotel and dressed for dining out. Did I get it wrong?"

Tom's chuckle didn't reassure her. The large twinkle in his eye implied he was plotting something as he said, "No I was trying to think of something different. Somewhere where we could both have a bit of privacy and could talk to each other without the world knowing what we were saying." He turned off the main road and they were driving towards the mountains and lake. "Between your friends and my family we could be starring in a conspiracy film."

At her tense glance he said, "Ally relax, this is one new friend taking another one out to dinner, no funny stuff. I promise to be on my best behaviour and I will give you the keys of the car if you wish so you can leave me whenever you tire of me or this whole idea."

"Now you are making me curious. And I have to ask, what is that smell?" Turning her head left and right she caught the faint whiff of lemon and oranges.

"It is dinner." Tom turned into a narrow gateway and they bumped down a long narrow driveway towards a steep bend. As they rounded the bend she gasped at the spectacular view.

Tom was delighted at her reaction. He couldn't have ordered a more perfect evening. The sun was setting behind the top of the mountain, casting a fiery glow, which raced down the mountain slopes and hit the dark water of the lake. "A beautiful and perfect scene", was the way Ally would describe it to Elaine the next day.

Suddenly in the midst of this beauty, the car stopped. Ally frowned. There was no brightly lit restaurant anywhere close to the car. "Why are we here in a field?"

Getting out of the car Tom told her, that if she waited for a moment or two all would be revealed. Ally tensed wondering if he was a serial killer and she his next hideous victim to be tortured and mangled.

He was busy pulling things out of the boot of the car and looking up said, "Forgot I promised to give you these. Here you go, catch. " Closing the boot with a snap Tom threw the keys to Ally. "Dinner will be served in a few minutes." He was amused to see her expression when she caught sight of the setting for dinner.

The large white tent stood on what she presumed were the foundations of a house or a barn. Despite her earlier thoughts, curiosity got the better of her and she followed him.

Tom was crossing his fingers and toes hoping she would not hop in the car and abandon him. She noted he was struggling with the heavy box and bag he carried.

They walked in silence to the tent. Ally stopped and stood looking at the view all about them. "It's gorgeous, so pretty and very quiet. Maybe, it's a little too isolated."

His chuckle alerted her that she had got something wrong. "What?" She demanded spinning about to face him.

"Ok. Look to your right. Do you see that group of trees nestled amongst them is the most beautiful house I have ever come across. You can just about see a puff of smoke from its chimney." Tom then pivoted to his left and stared into the hollow below them with hand outstretched. "Down below me, there is a small jetty running out at that point and if you draw a line from me towards it, you can see the two cottages sitting side by side."

Ally stood for a moment looking at the cottages. Finally she said, "I wonder what it would be like to live in a spot like this. I forget how close we are to the mountains and lakes, it's just that I get caught up in the routine stuff and don't tend to venture far from home."

To her surprise he said, "I love this site. I can imagine a house here, can't you? Though I am hopeless at figuring out where everything should go."

Ally considered the whole aspect of the site. "Considering the way the sun rises and falls. I would have the kitchen cum living room as one huge open plan room running the length of the house. I would have folding doors leading out onto a patio."

Tom considered her plan and asked, "why not decking?"

"Too much maintenance, ask Elaine she is always giving out about theirs. I would have the master bedroom as a dormer to the back and two others at the front with a shower room nestled between them. The hall would be small and leading off it a bathroom, a utility room and perhaps a study. That would be enough to keep any family happy here. What do you think?"

Tom nodded his head in agreement. "Sounds interesting, practical and beautiful but I will consult with you again in the future if the house ever gets as far as being built."

The words popped out of her mouth, "this is yours?"

"Such as it is, yes. I bought it some years ago when times were better, when I dreamt of living here with a wife and children but as you can tell, not only the business bubble burst but the dream as well." His statement was cool but his eyes betrayed him.

She wondered who had hurt him. Ally didn't want to have to deal with this now. She believed he was the heart breaker in his past relationships. Having that idea flipped about gave them something else in common. Logic pounced reminding her that everyone has their heart broken at some stage in their life. She heard herself say, "shame, it's such a beautiful spot."

"True it is, but it can wait. Mum's illness reminded me what is important in life, people. I would sell this in the blink of an eye if it meant I could have a life with someone I love." His eyes were fixed on her and Ally found herself with a thousand questions popping into her mind but before she could ask one of them the moment passed.

With a smile he said, "I should prepare madam's dinner if she doesn't mind me leaving her for a moment. I'll get you a drink so you can enjoy the view." He returned with a chilled glass of wine and a chair, which he set down for her. She watched as he fussed about placing the chair in the right spot.

Then he retreated inside the tent. A stray thought flitted into her head and she did her best to ignore it, 'he is still harbouring an optimistic view of a future for us.'

49. Dinner and a Whiff of Romance

Minutes later Tom announced, "Dinner is ready, madam."
Then he stepped forward and held back the flap of the tent.

Ally feeling more than a little curious stood and went to join him. The tent was bigger than it appeared. A heater sat in the middle of it. A table set for two complete with cutlery and glasses took centre stage.

"Wow it is huge. I thought when I first spotted it that it was like the one we used to camp out in during the summer holidays."

Tom held up a bottle of red wine in one hand and white in the other. Ally pointed at the white. Opening the bottle he asked, "Where did you go? Somewhere exotic, I suppose?"

With a chuckle she confessed, "The back garden. The tent was bought for me and Elaine. I think the intention was to give dad some peace and quiet. Don't think it worked as Elaine doesn't like creepy crawlies."

Sitting down and taking a sip of cold wine Ally began to relax. Tom asked her other questions about her childhood as he set a plate of salad before her. Ally glanced down at her plate. It was a work of art, a Greek salad waiting to be tasted. She stared at it and he wondered if he should have brought something else, "I could rustle up something else?"

Ally thought he was joking until Tom lifted the lid of the cool box which sat on the floor beside him. It was crammed to the neck with fruit and salads. "Are you planning on staying here forever? What's with all the food?" She teased him, "Or is this a kidnapping?"

He blushed. "I was so intent on getting this right I decided to bring extra vegetables and fruit in case you didn't like any of it."

"Relax. I love ninety nine percent of food." Ally began to eat. After a few mouthfuls she said, "Even if this wasn't great, which it is, I suppose dessert could redeem you."

"Depends if you like Tiramisu or chocolate mousse?"

"I think I've died and gone to heaven." Ally put her knife and fork down. "Tell me about your parents, I know your mum and she is an amazing person but no one ever mentions your dad, can I or should I ask, why?"

Taking a deep breath, he told her of how his dad believed he could do anything and that included having girlfriends outside of marriage. His mum tolerated him for the first five years of their marriage and then left him.

Ally's respect for Tricia magnified immensely as she could not imagine how a young woman with no income or means of support would take on moving out of the family home and creating a life from scratch with three young children.

When she said so to Tom he merely beamed at her, "I suppose she managed, as you do with the dogs."

"Hang on you can't compare a few dogs to three noisy kids. Dogs are dogs they are not noisy boisterous unpredictable demanding kids. I can't imagine having two Chloe's in a house never mind three? It would be like dealing with three goldfish with legs."

"But, they would be cute goldfish with legs." He teased as he lifted out a huge dish covered in tin foil. He removed the lid saying "I hope this pie isn't too cold because we have no way of heating it out here."

"And I thought you were organized Tom." The smell was delicious and Ally was surprised to see it was almost nine o'clock. She didn't hesitate to try the pie and the baked potatoes he had brought with it. The wine was her favourite and she asked him how he knew then answered her own question just as quickly. "Elaine!"

He nodded and poured her another glass while he made do with a coke.

She sighed. "How come a man with so much culinary talent hasn't been snagged by a tall leggy blonde with a generous bust?"

"Maybe it has to do with the fact that none of the above nameless women were interested in dating a man who spent most of his time outdoors. Ask mum or either of the sisters."

"It must be nice having sisters." The words popped out of Ally's mouth before she realised it.

"No, irritating is a far better way of putting it. And they were great at annoying and teasing me." For a while he opened up and related how many times he had been duped into introducing both girls to potential boyfriends. When he began to make a little money from the enterprise, it was soon stopped when his mum learnt of his endeavours. At her mystified look he explained further, "I was fourteen but played soccer with older boys. Caroline was fifteen and Sarah was twelve."

50. A Ruined Frock

The light was fading and the temperature was dropping. They were unaware of anything until they heard a rustling noise followed by a definite bleating sound.

"Sheep," Ally declared with a puzzled frown. To her horror one entered the tent, then another and another. The invasion took mere seconds. They were surrounded by bleating, pushing, inquisitive sheep. The animals investigated the cool box and its contents, sending food flying in all directions. Ally forgetting she was not wearing boots moved quickly out of their way onto the path near the car. She bumped into more sheep and lost her balance. She fell with a dull squelch into a nice soft mucky spot. Her flying body only served to startle the animals and they hurtled past her searching for a clear path to fresh grass.

Her good humour evaporated as soon as she felt the muck seep through the thin dress. There was no sign of Tom. "So much for a knight in shining armour," she muttered as she hauled herself to her feet. Catching a glimpse of him attempting to clear the field of sheep set her lips twitching. "I'm coming Ally, don't panic." His voice reached out to her.

Humour took hold as she watched his attempts fail over and over again. He set the herd into a panic around him. They began to move like a whirlpool hindering all attempts to move them on. She sat on the boot of the car laughing at him. His look of disgust soon sobered her and she went to help.

By the time they finally shooed them out of the field and into the next one both Tom and Ally were feeling mucky and tired. Her shivering caught his attention. Tom started the car, "you sit in here and I'll see what I can rescue then I'll drive you home."

Ally opened her mouth to protest thinking it would be quicker with two of them but she decided against it. She didn't want to be seen to be saving him, again. So she waited in the car. It didn't take Tom much time to clean up the remains of the picnic. Shoving the box and basket into the boot he got into the driver's seat without saying a word. Driving towards the road and watching for any lingering sheep he was surprised to hear Ally giggling.

"What's so funny? Really Ally any other woman would beat me around the head with the largest stone they could find. You are," he smiled as he slowed the car at the entrance to the site. The main road was quiet and she wondered what he was waiting on.

Her heart began to hammer as his intention became clearer. Leaning across the seat he gave her the lightest of kisses on her cheek. "Thanks. I am sorry about your beautiful dress. I am also sorry you didn't get to finish dinner. I will pay for the dry cleaning." He told her as she remained silent.

Ally was unable to think. Her face tingled where he had kissed her. She should be mad at him. Trouble was, it was hard to be angry with someone when they continually gave one hundred and ten percent in every little thing they tried to do for you. Staring out of the car window she couldn't help but wonder, "Was dessert nice?"

He chuckled. "Better than nice, stupendously spectacular I should say as I made it from start to finish."

Ally bluntly asked, "Is there anything you can't do?"

Tom slowed the car down and stared across at her. "I think we both know the answer to that. It is, yes, I can't be your boyfriend." He looked nervously at her.

"True but you are a good cook."

"I'm insulted by that remark. I'd say I am a terrific one and more handsome than the average chef."

With a shake of her head she said, "Can't deliver a final verdict as I didn't get to have dessert. As for the handsome bit, the jury is out."

Glancing over at him she saw his expression change to a warm relaxed smile. A warning bell rang in her head. She pushed it aside doubting if he was reading too much into one evening of mayhem and fun.

"Delighted to hear you don't go by appearances alone. I did when I was much younger. I put great faith in looks and look where that has got me, old, single and living with mother."

Tapping him lightly on the shoulder she informed him, "I know of someone who can help you design catchy posters to advertise your availability."

For a while he drove in silence. Ally was happy and muddy which did not make any sense to her but for once in her life she didn't attempt to analyse it to death. As they saw the welcoming lights of the town before them, Tom asked, "Your house or mine? Sorry, mum's?"

"Mine please I need a shower and a good strong mug of coffee."

Tom concentrated on driving the remaining way and the silence was not the least bit disturbing much to Ally's amazement. She had always felt in the past especially with John that silences were dangerous territory and nothing good would come of them. Tom was easy to be with she decided and tried not to question why she believed this to be true.

51. Sneaky Dog Business

The shrill ring of Tom's phone cut through the night. He glanced at Ally, "Please answer it for me."

Ally obliged. Before she could say a word, a familiar rough voice hurtled down the phone, "Tom, it's Steve. I thought you needed the money and the business. You buy her dog and I pay you. A deal is a deal. I need an answer by morning or..."

Steve ended the call. Ally was clutching the phone. She felt a cold chill swept through her. She swung about in her seat to face Tom. His eyes were not on the road but on her face. The car swerved into the path of an oncoming car and the loud blast of a horn reminded him where he should be looking."Ally, I can explain."

When she didn't answer, he tried again. "Ally, say something."

Ally's voice was cold as fury bubbled within. Her words spilled from her, "I suppose he was a business associate or friend of yours? Steve, why does that name ring a very loud bell? It seems he is not happy. You haven't kept your end of the deal and bought the dog for him. Tell me Tom how much money did it take to persuade you to ask me out?"

Her words hit him in the stomach. His worst nightmare was happening at this very minute. He had planned on telling her the truth tonight over dinner. From the time spent with her and Elaine he just knew he should tell her the truth. The untimely interruption by the field of roaming sheep ended his plans. Gripping the steering wheel tightly he swung the car to the side of the road and put the hazard lights on.

When Tom didn't answer she continued. "I suppose I should be flattered, you were going to offer me a great deal of money and be relieved your interest in me was purely business."

"I planned on telling you the whole story this evening. Of course you won't believe me now." Clearing his throat he looked at her. "I was approached some time ago. Steve needed a lead dog. His own dog is not able any more. He asked me if I approached the owner, and bought the dog he would pay me well for acting as the middle man. I stupidly agreed." Tom rushed on, "But I did not know the owner was you. I am sorry I ever listened to the man. This is the truth Ally. From the moment I met you, I knew I could never take one of your dogs away from you, besides you would never sell any of them. I understood that from the get go. I became lost in the maze of getting close to you. I rang him told him the deal was off but he wouldn't listen. I meant to call and see him but I forgot. You do that to me, make me forget what I shouldn't."

Ally couldn't hold back, she let fly with her fist and punched him in the shoulder. "So now you are telling me it is my fault."

"No, of course not this is my mistake from start to finish. I have messed up big time. I am sorry." He took a deep breath. She noticed his hands were gripping the steering wheel tightly. "I am sorry. I will spend the next ten or twenty years saying that to you if it helps convince you that I never meant to take any of your dogs from you."

A tiny bit of Ally believed him but she was madder than she had been in a long time. She wanted to get out of the car, to walk away.

"Can you take me home?" Ally felt sick, she needed to escape get out fumbling for the door handle she said, "No don't bother I'll walk."

52. More Bad News

Before she could utter another word or escape, he swung the car out onto the road and drove towards her house.

"I said I would walk." Ally could not look at him. She didn't trust herself to speak. History was repeating itself. Yet again, Ally was being drawn to the wrong type of man. 'I'm a fool and an idiot. I should stay away from them forever.'

They drove on in silence. The dark shadows of the night which had seemed romantic and pleasant only moments ago were now menacing and threatening. The car was moving too slowly for her. Tom swung the car onto Ally's road another loud ring of Tom's phone startled them. He was apologizing as he grabbed it. He glanced at the number and hit the brakes again. The car slowed to a crawl. "I am sorry I have to answer it's mum."

As soon as he heard the voice on the other end, he slammed his foot on the brakes. Ally peeped across at him. He looked frightened.

"What? Ok I'm on my way. I'll be there faster than an ambulance. Thank you." The second the call ended he turned to Ally who was out of the car and closing the passenger door.

"I'm sorry I have to go, it's mum she had a fall. A neighbour is with her. I have to go."

Her heart plummeted when she saw the look of terror on his face. 'It must be bad,' she thought.

Tom didn't hang around. He planted his right foot on the accelerator and the car lunged forward.

Ally opened her mouth. Her words, "I'll come with you," went unheard for he had already left. She watched the tail lights of the car grow smaller at an alarming rate and felt tears trickle down her face.

53. The Balance of Life

Shaken and upset Ally headed indoors straight to the bathroom. Shivering and coated in mud dropping her clothes on the floor as she went. She turned the shower setting to high as she stepped in. With the water pummelled her body, Ally tried not to think of the distressing phone calls. Twenty minutes later she emerged feeling a little human again but still cold. All of the stupidity of Steve and Luna was forgotten. Her main concern was Tricia, worse, memories of dashes to the hospital with her dad kept peeping through.

Clutching a hot cup of coffee she sat willing herself to be calm. She was frazzled and annoyed for not staying in the car. Reaching for the biscuit tin she tried to stop the vivid memories of Sam and his illness from tumbling about in her head. She knew better than most how horrible it was to get a phone call in the middle of the night.

Nights like this changed your life forever. She was tempted to ring him and see if she could help.

Ally groaned, she knew she wouldn't be able to sleep. The coffee and chocolate bar were not helping to calm her. As she tidied up she considered, again, if she should ring Tom to find out how his mum was but decided against it. Best leave it until tomorrow. She was climbing the stairs to bed when the mobile phone in her pocket started to ring. She answered it with caution.

His voice was panic stricken. "Ally, I got her here as fast as I could but.. But the doctors say it is not good. We thought she had a light cold but they say its pneumonia. It's the reason why she felt weak and dizzy. God I am so stupid, wrapped up in all of my own stupid life when I should have been there for her."

She didn't think. No one deserved to be alone in a hospital feeling useless with time dragging by. Her answer was brisk, "I'll be there in a few minutes." Putting the phone on speaker she pulled on the first pair of jeans and warm jumper she saw, then grabbing her bag was out the door hopping on one foot as she squeezed her left foot into the boot dangling from her hands.

54. Hospital

"It's just; she was doing so well and oh God what if." Tom's voice was breaking. His shoes squeaked on the hospital floor as he paced about.

She sought for a way to give comfort. "Tom listen to me, I will be there in a few minutes. Take a deep breath and talk to me, about your job, Mac anything. The doctors are with her. Panicking is not going to help, you or the doctors. You need to be calm though I feel a moron for saying it to you."

As she drove through the night on the well travelled route Ally concentrated on his voice. The last time she had been to this hospital had been to say goodbye to Sam.

It had been a horrible weekend. Sam had been fighting to stay with her but it was a battle they both knew he couldn't win. Ally hadn't left his bedside for two days. She was exhausted. The nurses persuaded her to go outside for a breath of fresh air. She was only outside two minutes when her phone rang. The tone of the nurse's voice had been enough. Ally raced inside to discover Sam had left quietly and without a fuss.

She rubbed the tears from her eyes. It was no use crying. She needed to forget her past and focus on the present. She couldn't arrive looking too upset Tom had enough to deal with.

Tom's voice was starting to calm as he related a tale of their first pet a rabbit they called Moron. It was also helping her to focus on Tricia and him. It would have been hard not to laugh at the stories for she could imagine them as children.

They must have been such a mad trio. She marvelled that Tricia had managed to rear them at all. It must have taken guts and courage. She said so to Tom telling him that a feisty lady like his mum doesn't give up at the first or second hurdle.

By now she was pulling in to the hospital car park. Thankfully the visitors had left for the evening and there were plenty of spaces.

'Just as well' she thought as she haphazardly abandoned the car. Tom was waiting for her in the hallway. His long legs were eating up the space as he paced about, running a hand through his hair. The bright glaring lights hurt her eyes as she absently reached out and used the hand sterilising lotion inside the door. His eyes were bright and tears had left a trail on his face. Ally's heart leapt as she went to meet him.

He stuttered sounding very unsure and unhappy. "I am sorry. I'm sorry for a lot of things but at this moment mostly for dragging you out, you were the first person I thought of. I couldn't call anyone else both sisters are away. I thought of you. I hoped but didn't expect that you might understand and come."

Standing on tip toe she put an arm about his shoulder with difficulty. She pulled him to her and she wished she could transfer strength and hope in a hug. When they broke free he looked lost. Ally took charge and led the way to the waiting room on the first floor. Tom walked beside her. He had shrunk to half his normal size. He looked frail. He was staring at the wall in front of them as they sat side by side. They were alone in the too brightly lit room. The heat was on full blast making it even more antiseptic and unwelcoming. Ally shuddered. Tom felt the tremor and turned to her, "Sorry for dragging you out and sorry for giving you a shocking evening, sorry for everything. I am so.."

"Stop saying that please," Ally interrupted sharply and felt his eyes boring into hers. "Of course I would come." She shuddered recognising the figure who was entering the room.

The nurse stopped in front of them, "Ally, how are you? It is Ally isn't it? I haven't seen you in a while."

Ally glanced at Tom. She saw the intense way he suddenly watched them. The nurse looked uncomfortable and Ally, squirmed a little in her seat.

"No, yes I mean it is me. I have been good. You know." Taking a deep breath Ally attempted to steer the conversation away from her and on to the more important issue at the moment; Tricia's health.

"This is Tom. His mum, Tricia Lynch, was brought in an hour or so ago, with pneumonia. I don't know which doctor is treating her or how she is doing." Ally looked at Tom.

He didn't hesitate and quickly gave the nurse the details. The nurse left them alone promising to be back in a few minutes with an update on his mum. Ally sat beside him battling with memories attempting to break through and upset her.

Tom glanced at her and noticed for the first time how upset she looked. He recalled the nurse's words and suddenly two and two made four. He silently cursed his stupidity for calling her. Taking a deep breath he leant across and clasped her hand. Giving it a light squeeze he searched for the right thing to say. "Thank you, for being such a good friend and braving the horrors of this place."

Suddenly things didn't seem terrible to Ally as she remembered the here and now. She was sitting here in company, not alone and terrified. She wasn't a frightened woman who had walked out on her husband six months previously and was awaiting the worst moment of her life. She was here to lend support to a friend whose sisters were on their way to join them. For the moment he was alone, he needed her.

Turning to face him she asked, "About Caroline and Sarah, what can I do to contact them?"

"Caroline and her husband had taken a much needed break." He sat upright, "as far as I know they are on their way

158

back. Sarah is working in London and is searching for a flight. So they will be here. I don't know how good or bad mum is and should I ring them and stop them or? It's the not knowing that is the worst, isn't it?"

A lone tear escaped and brushing it from her face Ally nodded, "yes but focus on how strong Tricia is" She searched for a distraction for them. "Remember how much she was looking forward to seeing you race against me again. It is becoming a running joke between us. I tried to bribe her but she refused."

"Oh," Tom looked a little interested. "A bribe to do what?"

"To over feed Mac and slow him up for our race." Ally smiled at him. For a few moments they simply sat. Ally hoped he was getting some comfort from her presence.

The whoosh of the sliding doors alerted them, they were no longer alone. Caroline stood before them looking upset but a little calmer than her baby brother. Walking over she embraced him and then briefly touched Ally's arm. "Thank you for staying Ally. This is my husband, Liam."

A huge bear of a man shook Ally's hand. He looked out of place and lost in this very warm small room. He sat on a chair next to Ally and then just as quickly stood up. "I'll find the true story about Tricia. Be back in a moment, anyone like coffee or tea though they both taste equally awful?"

At Ally's perplexed look as he left Caroline explained "he services the hospital beds, wheelchairs and all sorts of gadgets in here. Liam reckons he will find out faster than any of us what is going on."

Ally stood up and said, "Look, I am no good here to any of you. I should go, I could always pick Sarah up from the airport if needs be." No one got a chance to respond to this as the sliding door announced the arrival of the nurse. Stopping before Tom she gently began, "She is ill but the doctors say they are certain you got her here quickly enough. You can

159

come in and see her. She is on oxygen so I should warn you she will look and sound rough."

Tom and Caroline were on their feet in an instant. "We can see her."

"Yes, but only two of you for a few minutes."

Giving Ally's hand a quick squeeze Tom left holding Caroline by the hand. She waited until Liam appeared and then told him what happened. "Liam, I'll leave, now I know she is going to be okay. I can't do much for anyone hanging around cluttering up the place. Please tell Tom I'll take Mac back to my place so he doesn't have to worry about him."

Liam thanked her for being there for Tom and gave Ally his own phone number in case she had any trouble with Mac. With a sad smile she headed out into the dark night surrounded in memories old and new.

55. Helping and Waiting

The night air never felt so cool and welcoming after the heat of the hospital. Ally was thankful she had a job to do. When she got to Tom's house she discovered most of the lights on in the house and the back door wide open. Mac was barking before she got out of the car. Ally let him out saying, "Mac, looks like you are coming to mine for a holiday. Perhaps we should make it a working holiday." Ally was surveying the remains of his feeding dish as she spoke. From the look of it, he had used it as a football.

Mac trotted about the house by her side as she knocked off all the lights. With the house securely locked and Mac sitting in the back of the car they left.

Her dogs were delighted to see him and she simply opened Bob's kennel door and said, "Bed" Mac didn't hesitate. He ran in and sank into the spare mat she put in the corner of the kennel for him.

Ally was in bed ten minutes later but it took her another two hours to get some sleep. Trying not to think of Sam was keeping her awake so she gave in and remembered. When she could cry no longer she fell asleep for a whole three hours.

Next morning Elaine's questions about the date died on her lips, when she took a look at Ally's face she became frightened. Ally was the colour of snow with huge circles underneath her eyes.

"Do you want to cancel this morning?" Elaine asked.

"Thanks but sometimes you are better off just continuing on with your day. I will wake up in a few minutes and give you the whole story. It is a long one."

Elaine didn't utter another word merely went into the store room to collect the rest of the gear. After stowing the gear in the boot Elaine slipped into the driver's seat and saw to her delight Ally had brought two mugs of coffee for them.

Taking several large gulps Elaine left her cup on the holder on the dash and took a quick glance at the instructions she had received from the school. Slipping on her safety belt she began to drive. Five minutes later Elaine's worry was turning to fear for Ally because she had not uttered one word in the last fifteen minutes. Elaine reached over and rubbed Ally's arm, "Sure you are ok?"

Taking a deep breath Ally began at the beginning of her tale, telling where Tom had brought her for dinner, how nice, how special it seemed until the disaster of the invading sheep ended the evening.

Elaine didn't utter a word. She knew from the tone of Ally's voice there was worse to come. When Ally began to explain about the first phone call, Elaine merely murmured, "Oh Ally." Reaching out she gave her arm the briefest of squeezes. Ally nodded and continued on with her story relating all the gory details and her worries for Tricia.

Though she remained silent Elaine's mind was in overdrive. Sam's illness was imprinted on her mind. She would never forget the night he died. She had been stuck at home with a sick Chloe and no Ben there to baby-sit for her. Remembering it now she could still feel some of the guilt of not being there for Sam and Ally. She could imagine the turmoil that was raging through Ally. Being back at that hospital must have been a terrifying experience for her. Elaine also suspected that leaving Tom alone was playing havoc with her emotions.

Elaine listened for the next twenty minutes as Ally poured out her heart. When she finished speaking, she asked

Elaine, "You must think I'm crazy. Oh and I forgot to apologise about the dress but I will get it dry-cleaned."

It took Elaine a moment to catch up. Her mind was focused on the hospital. "Don't worry about that I would most probably have never worn it anyway. Or maybe Chloe might have got it as part of her dress up kit."

Risking a quick glance at Ally Elaine asked, "Did you have breakfast?"

It was typical of Elaine to think of someone's welfare in the terms of food. Sam used to groan when he saw Elaine coming into the house because he knew she carried another few of his favourite dishes. Understanding that this was her way of helping Ally raised a smile, "Thanks Elaine don't worry. I won't collapse. I had a small bowl of cereal though, I admit I am famished. Cooking anything even coffee was beyond me this morning. I rang the hospital, they told me Tricia is doing ok. Trouble is I feel useless."

"I know. I remember. It wasn't so long ago." With an apologetic look Elaine continued, "Sorry I don't want to stir up the past. But just walking through that doorway would give me the heebie jeebies. Why didn't you just come back to me? Afterwards, I mean. "

"You had enough on your plate, Ben, Chloe and Fred besides I had Mac with me."

"Don't mention dog's today particularly the new addition to the family - a shoe chewing, settee sampling Fred."

When Ally failed to pass comment on this Elaine let the topic drift. She was pulling into the schoolyard now and she knew that if anything could help Ally it would be a class or two of noisy boisterous kids.

She was correct. They helped to distract Ally and keep her preoccupied but as soon as the bell for break sounded she went outside to phone Tom.

"She is doing ok thanks for ringing me." Tom sounded tired.

Ally reassured him Mac was behaving himself like a true Irish gent, nicking the most food, grabbing the most comfortable bed and being romantic with the ladies.

Tom chuckled. "Thanks again Ally. It's great not having to worry about him or the house."

Mention of the house reminded her of the night before. She let him know she had secured it and had the spare set of keys. After assuring him she didn't mind keeping a watch on Mac and the house she hung up.

56. Progress

On entering the empty staff room Ally went to make a mug of tea telling Elaine about Tom's phone call as she worked. Then lifting her nose to the ceiling she said, "I feel a bit better after hearing Tricia will be ok. Do you know what? I am starving."

Elaine opened the small lunch box and divided the sandwiches she had brought with her between them. Munching on a sandwich Ally began to talk about the class they had worked with and suggested changes to the programme for the next class.

Any plans for the afternoon where put flying from her mind when she returned home and saw Mac had given a lesson to the others on how to dig their way out of the garden. Luckily for her they didn't share his enthusiasm for endless digging and no one had escaped but there were huge holes along the fence line. Clumps of grass and earth were scattered about the grass. Ally couldn't afford the luxury of calling it a lawn. With a sigh, she set about solving the problem. She loaded up her wheelbarrow and went to repair the damage. All of this was watched, with interest, by the chief culprit.

"You have been spoilt, we need to remedy that," she told him. Ally called the others to her and let them loose in Sam's training field at the back of the house where she had an assortment of footballs and tug ropes scattered about. An hour later her task was complete, the holes were filled and cordoned off with chicken wire to discourage any further digging. Hunger called as she headed indoors. Armed with a giant ham and tomato sandwich along with a mug of tea Ally sat looking out of the kitchen window. She felt tired, drained of energy.

"Worrying over Tricia's health is stupid. I know I have no control over it," she muttered as she washed her plate and mug. She debated ringing Tom but decided against it. Instead she rang Elaine to check on Chloe and Fred. The phone call to Elaine and Chloe perked her up. Ally shoved Tom to the back of her mind for an hour or two.

The next day her niggling annoying anger over the Steve O'Connor incident evaporated. Her reasoning was simple, everyone makes mistakes. Ally knew this better than most. She found her thoughts drifting to Tom on a regular basis. She knew he was busy visiting Tricia in hospital, looking after his job and the house. However she hoped for a phone call.

The call she received from Caroline surprised her. Caroline insisted Tom, was not hiding from Ally, merely busy and the purpose of Caroline's call was to ask Ally to mind Mac for a few days more. She didn't mind keeping Mac but he was a constant reminder of Tom who appeared to be avoiding her.

Ally kept an eye out for Tom wherever she went, on the routes to and from schools. After she wandered into the local football grounds to see if she could see either of the twins to get word about Tom she decided she was a fool. It was the dogs he was interested in and not her.

So she attempted to concentrate on getting Mac to behave. Mac was coming around to the Ally way of thinking. He was headstrong and smart but she enjoyed the challenge.

She had decided to focus on the battle with John over the rent. Ally had been dithering about making contact with him but in the end she didn't have to ring him. To her surprise it was John's girlfriend who solved this problem.

She was hosing down the yard when her phone rang. Ally answered automatically believing it would be Elaine on the other end. "Hi. I was thinking about changing our schedule." Ally began and got no further.

"Sorry, Ally. It is Ally isn't it? I think we should talk. This is Liz. I am the woman who..."

It was Ally's turn to interrupt, "Yes I know who you are. John explained."

Liz sounded annoyed and a lot older than twenty eight. "I wish he would do some of that to me. I overheard a conversation with his solicitor regarding the house a few days ago. Well, I agree with you, it would be simpler for everyone if we were to buy your half."

Ally was winded. She didn't expect this. "Sorry Liz did I hear you correctly? You and John wish to buy my half."

"No. That is my problem not John just me. It makes perfect sense to me. Why rent? We are both working. I can afford it. It will also prove to everyone how committed we are to our relationship."

Yes, it will Ally thought and hoped Liz was correct in her assumption about John. They spoke for a few minutes about some belongings of Ally's that were still in the house. Then after assuring Ally that their solicitor would be in contact with hers as soon as possible, Liz quietly ended the conversation.

Ally felt as if a weight had been removed from her mind. She could concentrate on looking to the future.

57. An Apology

The next thing on her agenda was to forget about Tom.
Obviously he had decided to forget about Ally. She speculated
on how easy it would be for him. He could pick a new woman
from his bunch of adoring fans. All of this was working its
way through her head while she peeled potatoes for her dinner
when Elaine arrived.

Elaine took the knife from her."Stop stabbing the potatoes
and spill the beans. Why are you looking angry?"

Ally handed over the knife and stepped to one side.
Leaning against the counter top she said, "I am feeling mad
because Tom has not made any contact with me in the last few
days, despite me having Mac here. He says we are friends
but."

Elained tried to reason with her. "You were the one who
told him there was no future in it for you or him. And now that
he has accepted it, you sound really childish and miffed."

Ally crossed her arms. "Do not!"

"Do too." Elaine smiled and punched her lightly in the
shoulder saying, "You should ring him."

When Tom rang shortly after Elaine left Ally suspected
he had been prompted or pushed into making the call. He
sounded tired. Ally automatically thought Tricia was ill again.
When he reassured her that was not the case, there was silence.
Clearing his throat Tom tried once again. She knew this was a
tough phone call for him but she wasn't going to make things
easy for him because of the Steve and Luna stupidity.

"I rang to see if I could call over. I owe you a lot, a big thank you for minding Mac, dessert and money for the cleaning of your dress."

"Oh," Ally hesitated, just a fraction. "Don't be silly you don't owe me anything. I'm just happy Tricia is on the mend."

Before Ally could say another word he told her not to move.

One minute later the frantic barking told her he was outside. She walked out to meet him and found he was being slobbered on by everyone of the dogs. Ally smiled and rescued him with a short sharp whistle. When Mac responded as quickly as the rest, Tom applauded her.

"Hang on I was afraid to bring this in, in case they got to it." Walking back to his car he lifted a huge box from the passenger's seat and said, "I brought this for you. It is a thank you present for helping me out. It was terrific of you. I won't ever forget it." His eyes softened and his stare was intense. Ally felt her heart melt. With difficulty she focused on what he was holding.

"There is no need but thank you. Let's call it quits." Ally lifted the lid on the cake box and discovered a luscious Mississippi mud cake. It smelt of toffee and chocolate. "We will need to test this immediately." She turned and walked into the kitchen. Once there she put on the kettle and pulled down mugs from the press. Tom was silently waiting for her to finish.

When she looked up, she saw he was watching her.

"I also owe you an apology for getting a little amorous on the night of our dinner. We agreed to be friends and I in my stupid male macho manner tried to take it to the next level."

Ally wanted to tell him there was no need to apologise. The way she saw it, there was two of them involved in this mix up. But why had Tom been avoiding her for the past few days? Did he think that by breezing in with a cake and a smile she would fall into his arms? Frowning she tried to silently reason her way through the rush of anger. She pulled out plates from

169

the press thinking it was a mistake to remember his absence had been more than a few days. It was six days exactly, she tried to reason how she could brush away six days of wondering and what if's, six days of him not ringing or showing any sign of recognition that she was living on this planet.

Picking up a knife she cut two pieces of cake for them. Her mind was working overtime wondering about his apology. Had Tricia coerced him into coming to see her? Did he really care at all? I mean, she silently reasoned, why apologise if he is really turned on by me? An explanation and a truthful one might help but an apology, oh, god that sucks. As she remembered the unforgettable kiss after lunch at Elaine's house, Ally felt colour rising in her cheeks. God, I am pathetic. I will not have one thought about him ever again.

58. Angels and Demons

Tom was staring at Ally wondering what the hell was going through her mind. He didn't understand her. He was trying but it was a hard thing to second guess what way she was thinking.

One moment she was sweetness and light and the next she was using that knife with a fierceness to terrorise any grown man. She was angry. He knew it wouldn't get easier if he didn't find out why.

'Better out than in,' he silently decided using one of Tricia's favourite sayings to them when they were moody teenagers. But trouble was she wasn't a moody teenager. She was an emotional woman loaded with all the intricacies belonging to her gender. And that meant trouble.

His voice was soft but his heart was thumping. He said, "Mum used to tell us it was far better to speak your mind than stay silent on the matter. Ally, will you please tell me what is going on inside your head?" The moment he spoke he knew he had made a bad move.

Ally's eyes didn't radiate sweetness and light. They were like a thundering waterfall sending sprays of fiery light showering onto him. He stepped back. She stood and pointed a finger at his broad chest. "You apologised." She stated. He nodded his head.

"But why?" she demanded.

'She has got me there' he thought. He knew there were many reasons why he should apologise. He struggled to pull the correct one from the messed up bundle of ideas flying about in his head. He gave a shrug preparing for the onslaught about to fly his way.

"Did you not feel it was right to kiss me? Did you not want to take it a step or six further?"

Tom was trapped. He knew whatever he said would be wrong. "I was trying to apologise because I overstepped the agreed line."

"And did I not in turn step over the line? Did you not feel it? Were you merely playing with me? God I am so stupid." She stared at him. "Before you arrived on the scene my life was less complicated. Now, I am feeling mad, angry and stupid."

"Ally what would you like me to do now? Apologise again. This time which apology is the correct one? My apology for apologising because I value your friendship and do not want to wreck it? Or should I apologise for my lack of insight into the workings of the female mind? "

The sound of his rising voice startled her. "What?" she asked.

Tom was angry. Anger was an alien emotion to him. His face was becoming red. He had made a stupid move. Too late he knew there was no way out of it. It was hard to reason with an angry woman but harder still when she made him so angry he was in danger of forgetting his name. He could try and save his dignity but hell he was tired of pussyfooting around a woman who said no but the moment he kissed her she demonstrated more than a hint of hunger for him. She deserved a bit of confusion.

He took a deep breath. It didn't work. Ally was normally lovable. He was standing before a woman who looked demonic. It might be a good time to turn and run but what was the possibility of holding his dignity intact and surviving a run to the gate?

As he stood there wondering how to be a hero and save the day he could only hear his hammering heart and the steady ticking of the clock. As he struggled to find the correct words she picked up her mug and left the room.

'Great Tom, the argument has left the building, what the heck do I do?' He washed his mug and the plate even though they were clean. Then he sat down and put his head in his hands. He was tired of, chasing someone who had no intention of getting caught. Tom was tired of being on his own and really worried about his mum.

He envied Caroline and Sarah who were both in a stable relationship. They could return home and moan or give out to someone who would talk and advise them. Mac failed sadly in that department. Glancing out the window at Mac, he was tempted to leave him with her. But the moment he stepped outside the sparkling eyes and wagging tail aimed at him won Tom over. Catching Mac's collar he said, "We should get out of here, buddy. Let's go."

59. Tricia Speaks

Tricia surprised Ally five days later by visiting her and being very honest. "What has happened Ally? I know something has, because every time I ask about you, he scowls, and disappears before I can ask again. Worse, he has a face like a wet fish. And let's be honest having one of those around you day and night is not a comfort or a pleasant experience."

"Tea or coffee?" Ally asked noting the way Tricia dropped her handbag and coat on a chair implied the older woman had no intention of leaving. She tried not to think of that miserable scene and how she felt afterwards but her mind was raw after the incident as it came flooding back to her.

From her perch on her bed, Ally had watched him leave. Tears tumbled down her face but she had no idea what had got into her. She had driven him away. And she had few friends in this world, she needed them all. At this rate it will be me and the dogs.

In the next few days she discovered she could cope and not think about him too much if other people did not ask about him or his mum. While walking the dogs the next afternoon she was stopped by one of the elderly gents who witnessed the race on the path, "when are you going to race your young fella again? Next time I believe he will give you a run for your money. I reckon you should do it for charity." His piece said he strolled away from her.

Tricia's voice broke through her distress, "A glass of water would be great thank you. I'm supposed to be drinking lots of the stuff and swallowing loads of pills." She grimaced.

Sighing softly Ally handed a glass of water to Tricia. "I messed up. I'm not sure how I let it happen. I've been trying to sort it out in my head but it's confusing."

Tricia smiled. "Love always is. Take Caroline for instance. She loved sports and was too busy competing to find a boyfriend. It was getting to the point where I was becoming worried, not that I would mind if she was gay. But then she was invited to play at a mixed football match for charity and the big lout she was marking got a lot of bruises from her. Liam must have a high threshold for pain because after the game he asked her out. And that was that."

Ally was grinning broadly. "You are joking, she literally beat up her future husband."

"Yes and she wonders why he isn't romantic?" Tricia changed the topic abruptly. "The real reason why I came was to ask a favour of you."

Ally didn't hesitate as she gave her answer with a quick nod of her head.

"Please talk to him." She took a deep breath and rushed on, "I know he cares for you everyone does even Robert and Owen. He is a man. I know it takes two to make a mess and two to clear it up. But if we wait for him…well."

It was hard not to smile at this strong independent woman who loved her children fiercely. "Aren't we supposed to be looking after you?" Ally wondered aloud adding, "How did you come here?"

Tricia answered with a smile, "Spaceship, how else? You are as bad as the others. They would wrap me up in cotton wool. I need to feel alive. I get so sick of hospitals, tests and worse still waiting for the results." As she spoke Tricia became aware of a change in Ally's demeanour.

Ally was remembering how little help she had been to Tricia. She looked uncomfortable. "I'm sorry. I haven't been much help to you or Tom, have I? All I've done is cause you worry and that is the last thing you should be doing."

Tricia confessed. "I have a problem - I tend to open my mouth without thinking. I'm sorry Ally I forgot you know better than anyone else. Did you know I had met your dad?"

When Ally looked surprised Tricia explained he had played with the Bridge group in the village hall. "He never let any of us know how ill he was until near the end. We miss him at all the old venues." Seeing the frown gather on Ally's face she elaborated. "He was always on the go. He helped form the active retirement group and became one of the chief organisers. He took us away on a few great trips, organised everything and was the life and soul of the party. But you know better than I."

Ally nodded and sniffed. It was hard for her when others talked about him but listening to Tricia brought memories of him flooding back. She wondered what advice he would give her. He had been full of patience with Ally and her mood swings. He coped, how she never knew with a house full of teenage girls, bills, working and housework.

Tricia got on to talking about more mundane matters and wisely didn't raise the issue of her son again. The only remark she made before she left was, "Since both girls are happy and settled, though Sarah isn't married, I often wish the same for Tom. When I was told the news about the cancer my one thought was I couldn't bear to leave him alone. He deserves to be loved, everyone does, especially you." Tricia then changed the subject to the twins.

They talked a little longer then Ally insisted she drive Tricia home. As they parted company, Tricia said softly, "You will sort it out. I know it deep down. It would just take one or other of you to take the initiative."

60. Tidy House - Tidy Mind

Ally spent the remainder of the afternoon catching up on household chores. It was all the stuff she hated, washing, ironing and most of all hovering. She continued until she was tired. Unfortunately she was not tired enough. Her brain was still flitting from the many what if's and possibilities concerning Tom and her.

At one point she stopped chasing cobwebs from the ceiling and muttered aloud. "There is no us, pure and simple. It's just me. I was a passing distraction. He will have moved on to another conquest."

This fact didn't cheer her. "I'm going to end up a horrible bad tempered old spinster." She told Luna who opened the door and brought the others in, Ally promptly shooed them outside again. She decided to take her present mood out on the state of the shower.

One hour later it was sparkling and could have been the feature in a television advertisement. Ally's energy reserves were depleted.

She went outside to the dogs and sat on the old wooden seat in the yard, beneath a starry sky for a long time simply petting each dog as they ambled by and sat with her. She was letting her thoughts ramble through her head like clouds. Not really focusing on anything until out of the blue she remembered what Sam used to tell her whenever she and Elaine fought. "Try and put yourself in her place, Ally. Look at it from the other person's point of view."

Ally sat there attempting to reverse roles. It wasn't easy more like looking through a fog of pea soup and seeing only what you needed to see. She needed to be blunt and honest. Ally knew if she could honestly see how she appeared to him then she might have a chance of working her way through the problem. Tiredness was getting the better of her. She decided she needed to sleep.

Stepping out of the shower later on Ally caught a glimpse of her self in the mirror. 'I look a mess,' she thought. 'Worse than that I know I am too competitive and perhaps this passion for my dogs is making me batty. She tired to find and focus on some of her better points.

I like my work with Elaine. I love kids and I adore animals. Here she stopped towel drying her hair and frowned. There wasn't much else on the good side. On the other side there was a mountain, I hate working indoors especially housework, I have no money, I have very few friends, I don't go out or socialise and I look a mess.

Ally went to bed having decided it was definitely time for a change.

61. Creating a New Start

Next day Ally surprised Elaine by suggesting they go shopping. Usually she shopped alone believing it should be done on a needs only basis.

Elaine was astounded by the request but happy to oblige. The following day the quest began as Ally called it, "to find the new me."

"What is wrong with the old you?" Elaine demanded of her. "You are sweet, fun and strong and very independent."

"And low maintenance, which is a very good thing from a male point of view." Ben added staring at his wife.

"Exactly low maintenance is what has me looking like a bag lady at the moment. I am only thirty five, not seventy five. In fact I know quite a few seventy year olds who look much classier than I do."

Elaine was busy scowling at Ben who retreated behind his newspaper. There was a football game starting at two and he hoped they wouldn't be back till late evening. Chloe never complained about him watching football, she considered the popcorn and the new knowledge she would gain about cursing a bonus.

When they arrived back at four thirty they looked tired but happy. Ben hoped Elaine's lack of shopping bags were a hopeful indication his credit card hadn't taken a beating. Ally had her hair cut and coloured but he had been told this was about to happen. She twirled about in her new cotton dress and coral sandals.

Chloe announced "I like the smelly stuff you have on Ally."

"You look hot," Ben told her.

Ally spotted Elaine winking at him. She smiled at Ben. "Thanks Ben only for your wife is present I would kiss you, for giving me the perfect compliment."

Ben glanced at his wife, "I aim to please. I would like it noted I can think for myself."

Elaine didn't let him away with that remark. "After ten years of living with me, you like any other dutiful husband should be trained by now, though it is often best to await further instruction."

Ally floated home an hour later. She supposed she should feel guilty about spending money on herself when the house badly needed help. It may be around far longer than me. That idea brought her right smack back down to earth.

During their lunch together Ally had told Elaine of Tricia's visit. Elaine in her usual forthright way insisted this was not only logical but a great piece of advice.

"Hmm. Stop running. Stop iffing and butting. Don't wait on him. You take control, get to know him better, then you can make a decision." Elaine turned her attention back to her lemon meringue pie.

Neither woman said another word about the dilemma until they were buying underwear. Elaine held up a very lacy white bra and matching knickers and repeated her statement "there is only one way of getting to know someone."

Ally blushed and turned away. Defiantly she picked up her plainer bras and walked to the till to pay for them. Elaine held on to the lace set and paid for it with her own bits and pieces. During the drive home Elaine house shoved the set into Ally's bag.

62. For and Against

Ally felt happier after her shopping trip. With chores done, dogs fed, she sat at her kitchen table and attempted to come up with a plan of action.

Grabbing a pencil and paper, she began her list. She scrawled, Ally's good points at the top of the page then added a huge question mark. The bad points were easy, broke, no full time job, grumpy and stubborn by nature, fixated on dogs, no culinary master class at this establishment - beans all the way.

She flicked back to the good side again. She was chewing on the end of her pencil. I don't have any, she sighed. She began to scribble without too much thought. I give to charity (when I have money) I help out at events, I don't drink, I don't smoke, I am quick to learn something new, I am kind to elderly people, babies and dogs – its all the others on the planet I have a problem with, and I don't collect a lot of girly stuff I will never use.

Ally considered the list before her. I sound like a nice person, except I am a little predictable which really translates as boring and too independent and stubborn for my own good. It was hard to admit it but she was no angel if she was honest, she would give her a measly score of six out of ten. I could be better she thought remembering the number of report cards that each teacher had scrawled that onto.

Out of mischief and because there was nothing worth watching on the television, Ally flipped the sheet over and began to list all Tom's good and bad characteristics. I need cheering up she decided. So I will do his bad points first.

Under the heading bad points, she wrote very slowly, he is too good looking for his own good. He is stubborn. Then she sat and stared at the white kitchen wall while attempting to find fault with him but she got distracted by the grubby state of her walls. I should really paint this room too brighten it up, she thought and turned her attention back to her real problem: Ally and Tom.

With a flourish of her pen she scribbled down good points and under the heading wrote, kind, kinder and kindest, romantic, likes dogs, good with kids in particular Chloe, which is an art form really, Ally decided with a smile. He is generous with his time and money she remembered the stories told by Robert and Owen about Tom taking them on holidays when they were younger and they didn't want to go with their mum and dad. All in all he is a ten out of ten guy. But....there lay the problem, he was too good.

Ally stared at the list. It didn't help. She was still frowning when the dogs wagging their tails and barking announced the arrival of a visitor.

Elaine jogged into the room followed by the pack of dogs demanding her attention.

"We have a problem. So I swung by to apologise. I am sorry I forgot I promised mum I would drive her and her best friend to the train station tomorrow. They are heading away for a few days peace. Though Mick insists he is getting the better end of the deal. Could you please cope on your own tomorrow with the class for half an hour?"

Ally forgot her list and focused on Elaine. "Of course I will." Elaine wearing her training gear, pink runners, pink neon running tights and a dark blue and pink top was stretching. "Elaine you won't be in danger of not being seen in that outfit." Elaine, she saw, had the decency to blush.

Giving up on the stretches Elaine sat and reached for the sheet of paper. "What are you doing? Is this to do with the new plans for upstairs? Let's see." Ally waited for Elaine's reaction.

Ten seconds into reading the list she did but not in the way Ally suspected.

"Oh my gosh. Congratulations." In her inevitable unique way of thinking Elaine leant across and hugged Ally to her. "Congrats you are actually facing up to it at last."

Ally prepared for another onslaught and lecture or at the very least questions. Elaine's words shocked Ally, "He is perfect for you."

Elaine jumped up and preformed a few stretches while Ally waited for more.

Frowning Ally asked, "Is that it?"

"Yes, tell me what decision you come to and we will argue then. I'm off. See you in the morning. He is a perfect you know what!"

"Rats." Ally thought so he is ten out of ten. Any woman would be mad not to jump at the chance of dating him or being romantically involved even for a short period of time. She pounced on her pen and under bad points wrote, "has to have several nasty habits or he would have been snatched by now." Feeling better that she could deduct a full point off him for his despicable smelly feet and snoring she went to bed.

63. Shocking John

Ally found it hard to sleep. After a restless long night, an early morning phone call from John didn't improve her humour. His tone was cool. He told Ally he wanted to meet her for lunch at one o'clock. Before he ended the call John said, "Alison, please do not dress as though you are walking the dogs."

Ally refrained from commenting. Conversation finished she walked into the utility room and kicked the laundry basket. It skidded across the floor. Feeling a little better she set off for work. It was a tiring morning and she did not feel like meeting John. She didn't tell Elaine about the meeting but she knew it was time to get everything in order. She was tired of burying her head in the sand.

Having said goodbye to Elaine and the room of panting children she raced off to the ladies room to work a minor miracle. Twenty minutes later she left feeling good. Her new dress and haircut were not steel armour but she hoped they would create enough of an illusion of confidence for her to knock the sarcastic comments into the back of John's throat, right where they belonged.

He was reading the paper when she entered the restaurant. It was a restaurant she had visited before. The waiter walked over to greet her complimenting her on how great she was looking. "Life must be treating you well," he said.

"Thank you, it is and it is about to get even better," Ally told him as John raised his head and caught sight of her. His eyes opened wide. Ally smiled this was better than she hoped.

When she sat down he said, "There is really no need to have gone to such great trouble for me," he looked her over as though she was on the menu. "You forget I have a beautiful girlfriend."

"Relax, this was not done for you." Ally told him as she focused on reading the menu. She picked out the first things she spotted on the menu. She wasn't fussed about eating as she didn't plan on staying long.

After placing her order with the waiter she turned her attention to John. Putting her menu aside she said, "John there is no point dilly dallying about this. So I will come out and tell it like it is - Liz rang me. We agreed on a lot of things. The main one being, one way or the other, you are going to buy my half of the house, you know it would be to your benefit."

His beady eyes were alight. "As I already told Liz, I have no intention of doing that. We will leave it to the courts to decide what to do about the house."

"No. We will not. You will buy me out. We will get an independent auctioneer to value it. End of story, pure and simple. Liz insisted she wants this to happen so I presumed, foolishly I suspect, you want the same."

Her answer knocked the light from his eyes. It was replaced with a cold steely stare. "How foolish of you both, you are assuming too much, Alison, I refuse to be forced into this."

"Speak to Liz, she is drawing up the agreement with her solicitor. It is no longer in your hands. We decided if you won't buy me out, she will."

His face became red with temper at this news. She could imagine how he would hate knowing Liz had equal share in the house. Luckily the waiter arrived with their starters. While he placed their meal in front of them Ally watched John. She was enjoying his discomfort. He never imagined Liz would have the courage to ring Ally and talk to her.

The real reason Ally agreed to meet him for lunch was to say it aloud. Let him know she no longer wished to have anything to do with him. Now Ally could move on with her life. With the house as good as sold and the divorce date set, she was free of him. Picking up her cutlery she began to eat. It tasted good and she was hungry.

John sat staring at her. She could feel his eyes on her. It was his way of intimidating people. She ignored him and enjoyed her lunch. A weight had been removed from her shoulders. Ally decided he had taken enough from her for too long. She would not let it happen again. If the new Ally was to survive life on her own, or with Tom, whatever happened would be her decision from now on.

She noticed John wasn't eating but she didn't let that bother her. His fingers were tapping lightly on the tablecloth. Ally ignored him. John aware he was being watched by the other diners, with curiosity, picked up his knife and fork to eat. With difficulty he answered the questions Ally asked him about his family. The waiter took away their plates and returned minutes later with their main course. Ally was keeping the conversation light and casual, asking about neighbours and mutual acquaintances. She was enjoying her beef stew but John's discomfort was the show stealer.

Finally he threw down his napkin, "I don't see how or why you and Liz should suddenly come up with this preposterous idea."

"It's a simple option. I think it is the best for everyone. It will suit you and Liz. I think you should talk to Liz first before blowing up and making a scene." Her comments were met with a cool stare.

He continued to stare at her. She knew it was a favourite trick of his to make people feel uncomfortable.

Ally decided enough was enough. If he couldn't be civil then she would have dessert at home in far better company.

Putting down her knife and fork she stood up.

Feeling calm she quietly said, "The bottom line is our life together is over. We have to start afresh and this is the best option, one that suits all of us. I no longer wish to hear from you John, good luck and goodbye."

Ally knew he had been winding up for a dramatic exit. She turned away trying hard not to smile. She had timed it to perfection. He sat there blustering and looking for a way out of this predicament while Ally calmly left.

64. Waking up to Life.

Ally became aware of a change in her outlook on life and in particular her future. This was highlighted after she witnessed a sweet simple scene on the main street in town one afternoon.

An elderly couple were walking side by side neither was speaking but they looked content and happy. She wondered why this was evident. She put it down to one simple fact, they were holding hands. The image lodged in her brain.

From that moment on she noticed the quantity of couples about her. Deep down she always knew people needed each other. She tried to hide from the question if she needed to be part of a couple but it kept popping into her head and finally she had to confront it. Her mum's early death followed years later by her Dad's illness and now Tricia's ill health all pointed to an annoying fact that no body knows how much time we have to spend on this earth.

Ally always believed she had wasted too many years on loving John. Their relationship had always been rocky and, she truthfully admitted to herself for the first time ever, they drifted into marriage. The result was two totally incompatible people trying to live two separate lives in one house.

Ally was struggling to sand the skirting boards in what would be a bright sitting or living room for her tenant while her mind played with the question of having a partner. She remembered her conversation with Liz.

A comment made by the younger woman had made her grimace at the time. "I know John can be stubborn and a little dominating but aren't we all? If two people truly love each other then they will tolerate the other person's horrid horrible habits."

'I never really loved John.' The realisation winded Ally, making her stop. We were young and foolish, wanting everything now.' She worked on, all the time considering if it was possible. An image of Tom popped into her head and she dismissed it.

Perhaps I haven't met my Mr. Compatible yet, she thought sliding along the floor as she sanded. Remembering Tom's futile efforts chasing sheep out of the tent made her smile. She conceded his preparations for the evening had been completed with great care to detail.

Then like a bad movie she couldn't remove the picture of him wet and miserable sitting on the banks of the river after their race. She put extra effort into her task. The sanding was done with in half the expected time.

Finished and relishing in the delight of being able to stand Ally walked outside to collect the cloths and white spirits. As she looked up at the sky the dogs gathered around and Luna began to nudge Ally at the back of her knee.

"Stop herding me, you minx." Ally told her.

The wind was light and the temperature rising. It was a perfect evening for a walk. Ally gave in to the hint she had been given and collecting a variety of leads and plastic bags set off for a short walk. She should have known better because somehow it became a long walk until she found herself standing in the field behind Tricia's house.

A cheery shout, "Hello would you like a cool drink" set the dogs racing off to greet Tricia. Ally groaned as she walked in through the back gate.

Tricia heard her. She chuckled and then whispered, "relax Tom is not here."

Within minutes they were sitting on the patio enjoying a cold drink. The dogs were busy partying with Mac. Bob lay at Ally's feet. For a while the two women sat and enjoyed the rare

189

warmth in the sun watching the fun and games going on before them.

Tricia cleared her throat and said, "without harping on at you or invading your privacy I will say I like the new look. I will add, it has been noticed by a certain nameless someone."

Ally grinned then said, "Good."

They sat like two Cheshire cats grinning at each other before Tricia spoke, "life changes so much but not always at the pace we want it to so my only piece of advice to you is choose the gear you wish it to be driven in and let everyone know."

Ally putting down her empty glass, walked to Tricia and planted a light kiss on her cheek, "when I decide what that is you will be the first or maybe second to know but thank you it is a great help being able to talk to you." Then calling the dogs to her she headed home.

She took the longer route back to her house allowing her mind to wander. Unfortunately for her it kept hovering over the subject of Tom. When she wasn't thinking of him, she was wondering where he was and what he was doing. She attempted not to dwell on the niggling question of whom he was doing anything with and if it was a serious issue.

What I need, she sighed, what I need most is a fairy godmother to help me solve all of my grotty problems at once.

65. Elaine Steps In

Next day indecision led Ally to vent her unusual humour on finishing sanding the window sills. "Nothing like hard work to remove all silly ideas from my mind" she muttered. The shrill ring of the phone interrupted her task.

It was Elaine asking if Ally could take care of Chloe that evening at her house. "I'll order Chinese or pizza for you to have for dinner, you would be doing us a huge favour please Ally. We haven't been out in ages and having the house to ourselves would be better than winning the lottery."

It would be ungracious to say no, Ally reasoned though she was tired and looking forward to watching an old movie after a long hot soak in the bath. "Yes love too. I promised Chloe ages ago, we would go to the cinema, so I suppose now is as good a time as any."

"Ahh thank you. I'll bring her over at half six, okay?" Elaine finished by thanking Ally and said goodbye quickly.

Ally didn't delay in finishing her sanding. She was tired and looking forward to having Chloe for the evening. 'You can get too much of this living alone stuff,' Ally reminded herself as she went to clean up. Ally pulled on a favourite, but seldom worn green dress and slipped on a pair of sandals before brushing her hair and declaring herself ready. "No point buying them and not wearing them," she told her reflection.

She was busy in the kitchen tidying up old newspapers and magazines when dogs barking and tyres crunching on gravel told her a visitor had arrived. Certain it was Elaine Ally walked outside. A Chinese delivery van was parked in the driveway. The driver handed over the bag of food and left smiling broadly because of the large tip Ally gave him. Carrying the bag she headed towards the kitchen and peeped inside it. She frowned. There was a lot in it for Ally and Chloe. She wondered if he given her the wrong order.

Setting the bag on the counter top in the kitchen she heard another car pulling up. Once again the dogs sounded the alarm and when they didn't stop Ally frowned wondering who her guest was. Her mobile rang, she grabbed it, 'hello.'

Elaine was talking fast, "Ally, promise me you won't be mad, don't shut the door in Tom's face. Talk to him. I ordered for two. He rang me a moment ago, he thinks you are going to kill him. Don't please." Elaine paused then added, "We are going to visit Tricia later. Tom doesn't need to rush back. You can both relax and take your time to sort yourselves out. And don't shout at me, Chloe is in bed at her best friend's house. I wouldn't like them to hear you shout all the way across town."

Temper rising and her tone of voice keeping pace with it, Ally wailed, "No. How could you? Elaine what have you done?' Elaine hung up. "Coward," Ally muttered.

Sinking into the chair Ally's heart hammered loudly in her chest. She wanted to run and hide but there was no way out. She tried to figure out the best line of action. If he came in she would have to face him, if he didn't then she was okay, she could celebrate by finding Elaine and throttling her. Even that didn't bring any sense of satisfaction because she realised she was leaving it up to Tom.

She sat for a while. Ally attempted to not think of who was sitting in her driveway. Ironically, her treacherous mind flitted with the idea of what it would be like to have him come trundling through her gates on a daily basis with a smile in his eyes just for her. The thought of this happening had butterflies fluttering in her stomach. She sat and chewed on her lip.

Money might make some people's world go round but Ally knew for her it would always be love.

She knew it was ridiculously old fashioned and a silly idea. Love is for keeps. This, she had always believed to be true which is why it had taken her so long to admit marrying John had been a huge mistake.

However Tom was not John he was the complete opposite.

John would have rushed in here full of confidence, certain that the decision was made, by him and for him but all under the disguise of being for them.

"Where is he?" she glanced at the clock and saw it was a ten minutes since he pulled in. She had not heard the door of the car slam or footsteps crunching on gravel. The dogs had stopped barking and were lying in the yard. Perhaps it was someone making a u turn in her driveway or had Tom driven away after deciding this was a bad idea.

Well she couldn't sit here all day. She knew there was only one way of finding out, by walking outside and taking a peep. Suddenly Ally made a decision.

66. Answers

Ally stood, fussing with her hands smoothing the hem of her dress. The second she was on her feet her bravery vanished. Looking for an excuse to stay indoors, she pulled scented candles from a press with her heart pumping so fast she was surprised it didn't explode.

She lit them with a tremor in her hand hoping she wouldn't burn the house down. The act calmed her. She began to think clearly. I need to do more than light candles to show him I have hope for the future, our future, she corrected. The strength of this belief surprised her gave her the courage to walk outside. Then her courage failed her. She stopped and stared.

He was sitting in the car, his head resting against the steering wheel. She raced out wondering if he was having a heart attack or ..? Ally stopped when she realised what was happening.

'He doesn't know what to do,' the fact hit her like a smack in the face. She stood watching him, urging him to make the first move. With her eyes boring into him she willed him to look up. When he didn't, Ally stepped backwards and hit against a flower pot sending it flying against the house wall with a loud thump.

Ally looked horrified at the shattered pot. She could feel Tom's eyes on her. The moment stretched. Finally she risked glancing at him.

She didn't want to look away in case he vanished. She knew what she should do. However, the memory of him storming out of her house came to her. Remembering their last meeting and the confrontation with him made her blush. She had exploded. Her fears and failures had poured out of her onto him. She had been unfair. Ally acknowledged she had acted like the biggest bitch of all time. Knowing she had reduced him to this state of uncertainty was not good. For a second she hated her sense of independence and John. Both were to blame for this fear of putting her life in another person's hands.

She knew if she didn't take this risk she could lose everything. There was the potential for years of happiness staring her in the face. If she chose to hide behind four walls and her dogs then she would have a life of loneliness and pretence.

And I am no good at pretending Ally admitted to herself. I am the worst liar in the world, whenever I tell a lie, I always get caught out. I have to face it I have been lying to myself. This is important. Tom is important to me. I want to include him in my life, every day or a life time. I want to take this chance. Wrong she thought I need to take this leap.

"You can do this, you need to take a chance Ally," she muttered stepping forward and going to the driver's door. Pulling it open, she extended her hand. His fingers normally so warm were cold to her touch. He looked puzzled.

He doesn't know how I feel, Ally realised. She hesitated knowing her next move would determine the rest of her life. She had no idea how to get it right.

I can't afford to mess this up she thought and stood looking at him. A thin thread of warmth reached out to her as she acknowledged the truth. I know what I want. The certainty which had filled her in the kitchen was back. Taking a deep calming breath Ally summoned up every last ounce of courage she had. She knew she was prepared to fight for him and them.

67. Solution

When Ally opened the driver's door Tom was surprised. He discovered he couldn't speak or move. Tom sat staring at her, noticing so many details they threatened to overwhelm him.

To him, Ally looked frail. The tell tale dark circles under her eyes worried him. He hoped he wasn't the cause of them. He had no wish to hurt her. He wanted to shout out his love for her. But a tiny part of him was holding back because he believed her when she said love would never feature in their lives. Worse, it would never be welcome in her life again.

He wondered if he could tolerate friendship. Would it be enough for him? That question had plagued him for the past few weeks and nearly driven him mad. She was all he dreamt of though he knew she was too independent to risk putting her life in a man's hands once again. How could he convince her it needn't be like that?

Floundering and needing advice he had turned to her best friend. Elaine's answer surprised him, "she needs you but hasn't accepted it yet. She knows this but her stubbornness is keeping her from admitting it, now you should be as stubborn. Go see her. And Tom, this time take your time."

Elaine was the third person he spoke to in the past hour. His state of indecision led him to look for advice. When he confessed why he needed to hear their opinions. Their answers surprised him. He suspected, Elaine, Tricia and Caroline were plotting and planning something but he didn't really care, he needed to know if he was right to come here today. He needed to hear it from her lips once and for all. If she wanted him to leave he would go quietly. Until now he believed she would never change her mind and at this moment he was building up the courage to find out if he was correct.

Ally stood before him and reached out to him. Her hand was warm and he was pulled from his car. "Ally," he started to speak and stopped. His heart was pounding but his head was reasoning, yet again, the reality of the situation. This was no happily ever after movie. In the movie the leading lady would swoon at his feet, he would scoop her into his arms and together they would ride off into the sunset. This was reality, where all mistakes and fears got in the way. And there was a lot, his blundering mistake with Steve O'Connor, the awful dinner, her divorce and fear about getting into another relationship, his competitive spirit, his failing business, his dreadful attempt at apologising and explaining how he felt. His list of failures was interrupted by Ally tugging on his hand.

"Please Tom come in." He followed her inside. He stopped to stare at the flickering candles and set table. Part of him took in the candles, the table set for two and wondered who she was waiting for but when he glanced back at her he noticed she was hesitant as though waiting for him to make the first move.

Ally stood to one side. He waited for her to speak.

A tiny flicker of hope danced in his chest and looking down at his hands he noticed for the first time they were empty. Abruptly he pivoted about and went outside saying, "Oh I forgot…"

68. A Door Opens

Ally collapsed into the nearest chair. 'I've made a fool of myself again, why do I do it?' was her desolate thought and tears gathered. She stupidly believed by bringing him indoors he might begin to understand how serious she felt, about him and their future.

Shaking her head she promised herself she wouldn't cry, again. Ally lost the battle as one by one in a steady trickle tears escaped. They threatened to turn into a torrent. Lost in her misery and self doubt she didn't hear him enter the room.

His soft tone of voice startled her, "Ally?"

Looking up she discovered she was staring at an enormous bunch of flowers. The blossoms were hiding Tom's face. Getting to her feet she pushed his hand aside, lowering the flowers to reveal his twinkling eyes. Elation soared through her then she realised Tom was talking to her. When she failed to answer he continued to speak.

"I know it's a cliché but I decided to risk it. I am happy I did. Please don't be upset with me, don't cry." He handed her the flowers. She stared at them and saw nestled deep amongst the roses, a child's toy, a sheep who was wearing Wellington boots. Raising her eyes to his she watched as Tom pulled a box of her chocolates from his pocket. Leaving them on the table he reached inside his coat and pulled out a bottle of wine. It too was placed on the table. Then like a magician he pulled out a large bag of dog treats. His smile was timid. "I was afraid to leave anything to chance. They might be a bit squashed by now, sorry."

Her words caught in her throat and she watched his face as she said, "You shouldn't have." Seeing the disappointment flit across his features she continued quickly, "I didn't need any of those, though they are beautiful. I just needed to see your face, not angry but smiling at me. I am so sorry. I have acted like a spoilt selfish bitch. Can you forgive me, please?" She grinned realising if he hadn't forgiven her then he wouldn't have brought half the contents of the flower shop to her.

This unleashed a fresh batch of tears. Nobody had ever bought her flowers, never mind chocolates and treats for the dogs.

Tom reached forward and gently wiped the tears from her face. Sitting beside her he simply held her hand and waited for her to calm down. When the tears stopped he leant in close to leave a trail of soft whispering kisses along her cheek.

"I'm an emotional wreck. Sorry." Ally whispered.

He pushed her away from him to look at her face. With his index finger he traced the outline of her jaw, "Just so happens I love emotional wrecks, in fact they are my speciality. My goal is to help you recover and find the balance to life's quirkiness." Bending down he kissed her lightly.

With a gulp of delight Ally leaned against him. She returned his kiss with one of her own. As their lips met she melted, her mind turned to mush all semblance of thought evaporated. She could do nothing as he quite carefully and tenderly tore down the last of her barriers with a deep tender kiss. Her hunger grew she became the driving force, looking for more from him. As lips touched and hands caressed they were lost in their private world. Tom was the first one to break contact pushing her gently away from him.

"Hang on. Earth to Ally. I need to check something. Are you sure you want this? My business is barely supporting me. I snore. I throw my dirty socks and clothes all around the bedroom. I often have snacks in bed and I sometimes have a dog for company in there too. I don't have a huge lifestyle or house to support you in the manner to which you are accustomed."

Stepping away she said in a prim voice, "you forget you are suggesting you mess around with a nearly divorced woman. Can you not wait?"

When he failed to answer she smiled, "Well I can't." Ally began to laugh and said, "as long as there is room for me and my five, we will be fine."

Still he held her at arm's length. "We need to talk. There is so much you don't know. So much I want to know."

To his surprise she chuckled, "we will have a lifetime to talk and argue, but not now."

All thought was lost as he pulled her to him and for once in her life Ally didn't pass any heed to the wagging tails of her dogs who watched at the window.

Made in the USA
Charleston, SC
29 June 2015